Disorderly Elements

Disorderly
Elements

Bob Cook

All the characters and events portrayed in this work are fictitious.

DISORDERLY ELEMENTS

A Felony & Mayhem mystery

PRINTING HISTORY
First UK edition (Victor Gollancz Ltd.): 1985
First U.S. edition (St. Martin's Press): 1985
First paperback edition (Methuen): 1986
Felony & Mayhem edition: 2006

ISBN-10: 1-933397-41-1
ISBN-13: 978-1-933397-41-2

Manufactured in the United States of America

To my parents

"One of these subtler minds is named, let us say, Wyman...Wyman's overpopulated universe is in many ways unlovely. It offends the aesthetic sense of us who have a taste for desert landscapes, but this is not the worst of it. Wyman's slum of possibles is a breeding ground for disorderly elements."

W. V. QUINE,
On What There Is

The icon above says you're holding a copy of a book in the Felony & Mayhem "Espionage" category, which features spies and conspiracies from World War I to the present. If you enjoy this book, you may well like other "Espionage" titles from Felony & Mayhem Press, including:

The Cambridge Theorem, by Tony Cape
The Spy's Wife, by Reginald Hill
Who Guards a Prince, by Reginald Hill
The Romeo Flag, by Carolyn Hougan
Shooting in the Dark, by Carolyn Hougan
A Gathering of Saints, by Christopher Hyde
The Labyrinth Makers, by Anthony Price

For more about these books, and other Felony & Mayhem titles, or to place an order, please visit our website at:

www.FelonyAndMayhem.com

or contact us at:

Felony and Mayhem Press
156 Waverly Place
New York, NY 10014

Disorderly Elements

PROLOGUE:
BUDGET DAY

THE CHANCELLOR OF THE EXCHEQUER stared through the front window of 11 Downing Street. He was uneasy. There was a large crowd of people outside. They did not look happy.

"Fucking rabble," he murmured.

"Pardon, dear?" asked his wife.

"Nothing," he grunted. He put on his overcoat and picked up his briefcase.

"I think it's going to rain," she said.

"Yes."

He opened the front door and stepped outside. He was greeted by a chorus of booing and catcalls. He replied with a broad smile and, in time-honoured fashion, he waved his briefcase. In a few hours the contents of that briefcase would be public knowledge.

Apart from the traditional attacks upon smokers of

tobacco, drinkers of alcohol and drivers of motor vehicles, the Chancellor had something nastier in store. His proposed cuts in public expenditure would make previous efforts look tiny by comparison. This time there would be no half-hearted attempts at penny-pinching. This time the public sector would be kosher-killed.

There were two special areas upon which the Chancellor wished to inflict Grievous Bodily Harm. One was the Civil Service, with its vast bureaucratic empire and obscure fringe departments. It was time for the complacent, public-school monopoly of Britain's administration to end.

The other target was education, in particular the Old Universities. In the Chancellor's opinion, these establishments fostered a brand of elitism that retarded the progress of the New Right. The Chancellor was a New Conservative. He fervently believed that all hope for the future of his country lay with the dynamic middle classes. The aristocracy of Oxbridge dinosaurs was a brake upon his party's ideological progress. They would have to go.

Of course, the Chancellor's background in a Secondary Modern School and his failure to pass the Civil Service exams had no bearing whatsoever on these views.

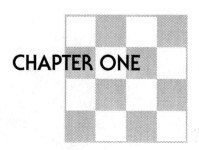

CHAPTER ONE

The second of May was a bleak, muddy sort of day. Michael Wyman splashed through last night's rainwater as he walked down London's Tottenham Court Road. By the time he arrived at his office on the north side of Percy Street, he felt as if he had finished his day's work. It was 9 A.M.

Wyman's office was a faded Georgian building which lay between Greek and Chinese restaurants. The large blue doors carried a sign which said "The Family Planning Association has moved to 32 Charlotte Street".

Mr Berkeley, the porter, greeted him.

"Good morning, Dr Wyman," he said, in a voice of habitual gloom.

Mr Berkeley was a religious man. He belonged to one of those sects which believed that Armageddon would come that afternoon at 3 P.M. His desk was littered with tracts, and he would give one to anyone who entered the building. As usual, he gave one to Wyman.

"Good morning, Mr Berkeley. Thank you," said Wyman. He walked up the stairs to the second floor and sat down in his office.

Berkeley's pamphlet, he noted, was a typical specimen. It exhorted its reader to repent before being done to a turn in the eternal microwave oven. Wyman was urged to abandon greed, lust, gluttony, blasphemy and deceit. He was then asked to donate £2.00 to the happy sect so that others could be similarly informed. Wyman threw the pamphlet into his wastepaper bin. A true religion, he reflected, should never ask for less than a fiver.

Michael Wyman was fifty-six and looked it. His hair was white and thinning. He had a pink, flabby face and a paunch that indicated a lifetime of comfort. His black spectacle frames were peppered with the dandruff that Vosene had failed to remove.

Despite all this, he was not an unattractive human being. He was good-humoured and kind. The only people not won over by his erudite charm were those who were neither erudite nor charming. Unfortunately, these included Wyman's employers and most of his colleagues.

Wyman worked for M16, the British intelligence-gathering organization known to its members as the Firm. He was stationed in a backwater known as the Department, which specialized in collecting information from obscure sources in East Germany. Once upon a time, at the height of the Cold War, the Department had been an important feature of British Intelligence. Now, however, the Department was as dry and dusty as those who ran it.

Although he worked in Intelligence, it would have been wrong to call Wyman a spy. He was a half-caste: a Ph.D. in Philosophy who had joined MI6 as an alternative to National Service. For the next thirty years Wyman had combined his career as a university don with that of an intelligence officer. The combination had not been altogether successful. In academic circles he was regarded as a wasted talent, and in MI6 he was deemed to be past his prime.

None of this bothered Wyman much. He was comfortable, and retirement was not far away. His college would give him a reasonable pension. He was secure, and had no worries.

Wyman's in-tray contained a number of letters, and he began his daily routine by reading them. The first was a memorandum from MI6 headquarters. It reminded him that his report on arms manufacture in East Germany was three weeks overdue, and asked that it be sent in immediately. Since Wyman had not yet written the report, he was in no position to send it in. The memo joined Mr Berkeley's tract in the wastepaper basket.

Just as Wyman was about to open his next letter, Mrs Hobbes knocked and came in.

"Morning, Dr Wyman," she trilled. "Cup of tea?"

Mrs Hobbes was the tea-lady, cleaner and general factotum. She was fat, hairy and cheerful. Her hair was styled in a blue rinse, and she always smelled of lavatory cleaner. Wyman speculated that there were flying ducks on the wall of her living-room and a plastic gnome in her front garden.

"Good morning, Mrs Hobbes," Wyman said. "I'd love a cup, thank you."

"Right you are," said Mrs Hobbes. "Shall I do your office today? It does need a clean, and Mr Berkeley's fixed the Hoover—"

"Not today, thank you," Wyman said quickly. He did not like having his office cleaned, even though it was a mess. On the very few occasions that Mrs Hobbes had ever tidied it up, Wyman had complained for months afterwards that he could not find anything. That was because Mrs Hobbes had an irritating habit of putting books on bookshelves, files in filing cabinets, and paper in stationery cupboards. Wyman found such efficiency disagreeable.

Mrs Hobbes went away to make the tea, and Wyman opened his next letter. It was from the Director, and was countersigned by Owen, Wyman's immediate superior in the Department.

He read the letter in disbelief, and then reread it to be certain that he was not hallucinating. The opening lines were standard enough nowadays: "Dear Dr Wyman, As you are aware, the last budget has forced us to implement severe economies", etc.,etc. It was the concluding paragraphs that hit Wyman like a punch in the face.

"Good God. I've been sacked."

CHAPTER TWO

THE CAFÉ ROMA IN PERCY STREET was run by an Italian called Giuseppe Peano who knew what good Italian food tasted like but found it more profitable to forget. Having abandoned his culinary integrity, Giuseppe made a reasonable living by serving spaghetti with chips and lasagne with baked beans. The only thing even Giuseppe could not bring himself to desecrate was his coffee. He served the best cappucino in London's W1.

Wyman stepped into the café at 11 A.M. and said good morning to Giuseppe.

"Good morning. Iss usual for the *dottore?*" Giuseppe asked.

"Yes, iss usual," Wyman said.

Giuseppe called "Cappucino" to a sultry girl behind the counter. She clanked metal cups, twisted chromium pipes and steam-blasted milk as Giuseppe went to Wyman's table.

"Perhaps you like to eat today, *dottore*?" he suggested.

"I don't think so," Wyman said.

"No? You no' hungry? No' want to eat? Why not?"

"Because I like Italian food," Wyman said.

Giuseppe laughed.

"Very funny, *dottore*."

"No, Giuseppe. Very tragic, from a gastronomic point of view."

Giuseppe shrugged.

"Perhaps," he conceded. "But, if iss what people like, iss what they get, no? All right, so iss sheet. People like sheet."

"I don't," Wyman said.

Giuseppe considered this as the girl brought the coffee. Then he said: "For you, iss only one solution. Marry nice good Italian girl who cook for you. Then you will be happy."

"That's an idea, isn't it?" Wyman said. "I'll think about that, Giuseppe."

"You no' too old. Nice good Italian girl give you cheeldren, not like these Eengleesh *scrofe*—how do you say *scrofe, dottore*?"

"Sows, Giuseppe," Wyman said. He was never entirely sure if Giuseppe was joking. "Ah, here comes my very own *scrofa* now."

Margaret walked in. Her cheeks were flushed with the morning cold.

"Hello, Giuseppe," she said. "Cappucino, please."

"Good morning," said Giuseppe, and he returned to the counter.

Margaret was opposite Wyman.

"Hello," she said. "What's new?"

"Lots," Wyman said. "How about you?"

"Lots," she said. "Who goes first, you or me?"

"Ladies first."

"Age before beauty."

"The Firm is making me redundant."

"I'm pregnant."

"Good God!"

"Christ!"

There was a long silence.

Margaret Ramsey was thirty-nine. She was tall, blonde and slender. Like Wyman, she was a divorcée. She had worked as Wyman's assistant until it became clear that she was assisting Wyman with more vigour than her job merited. At that stage Owen's embarrassed coughs had articulated themselves into an ultimatum: either Margaret would be transferred or she would leave the Firm. She chose to leave.

Margaret's resignation invigorated their affair. All the care and enthusiasm she had formerly applied to her work were now lavished on Michael Wyman.

"When did you find out?" Margaret asked.

"This morning. Nothing was said; just a buff envelope on my desk which said that the Firm has to economize. It was all very polite, of course, but the point was clear. They're getting rid of dead wood, and in arboreal terms, I am very dead indeed."

"But that's absurd. You do a splendid job for them."

"Tell them, not me," Wyman said. "Anyway, it doesn't really matter. What about this baby? How on earth did it happen? I mean...well, you know..."

She nodded.

"Yes, I know. The doctor was wrong, wasn't he? I am fertile, obviously."

"Are you absolutely sure about this? I mean..."

"Absolutely sure."

"Well, well," said Wyman. A roguish grin split his face open and he laughed.

"It's not as big a problem as it seems, you know," Margaret said. "I'll just fix things up with a clinic. I'll only be away a couple of days—"

"What? You don't want to have an abortion, do you?"

Margaret seemed confused.

"Well, I thought...I assumed that you...well, you know..."

"I know nothing of the sort," Wyman snorted. "If you don't want to bring up the child, I will."

"You want the child?" gasped Margaret.

"Of course," Wyman said. "Why shouldn't I?"

"I think I'm going to faint," Margaret said.

"Two more cappucinos, Giuseppe," Wyman said. When Margaret had recovered, Wyman explained his plans. "It's quite straightforward," he said. "I'll return to College and work there until retirement. The income isn't as good, but it's enough to manage."

"What about your alimony payments?"

"They will continue," Wyman said. "It's not as if I have a great deal of choice, though I suppose they might be reduced a little."

"A lower salary, alimony and now the baby. Michael, are you really sure you can manage all that?"

"I'll find a way. The College is quite good about these things."

"I hope so," Margaret said. "If they're anything like the Firm, we'll be in a real mess. Why didn't they give you a pension? It's the least you're entitled to."

Wyman sighed.

"I've explained this before. The arrangement with the College doesn't permit it. Officially, I was lent out to the Firm by the College. In theory, the College is my real employer."

"But they changed your status to Honorary Fellow."

"A technicality," Wyman said, waving his hand. "The fact is, no contract was ever signed by either side. It's a gentleman's agreement."

"In that case," Margaret said, "let's just hope that your College is run by gentlemen."

"It is," Wyman said. "There is one more thing..."

"What's that?"

"I'm not sure how I should put it...it's to do with how you, er...fit in."

"Fit in?" Margaret's eyes narrowed in suspicion. "Michael, are you trying to propose to me?"

He grinned sheepishly.

"I suppose I am. Not very good at it, am I?"

"No, you're not."

"Well, er...perhaps you'd like to think about it."

"I'll do that," she said solemnly.

"Jolly good. Heavens above, is that the time? I really must get back."

He stood up and fumbled in his pockets for money for the coffee. Margaret gazed at his obvious embarrassment in silence until she could restrain her laughter no longer.

Wyman looked at her indignantly.

"I fail to see any cause for laughter," he said.

CHAPTER THREE

"AND NOW," SAID THE MASTER, "we come to the final item on the agenda of Open Business: heating costs."

He looked round the table at those present. College Council meetings took place every fortnight during the academic term, and most of those involved found them insufferably dreary. When Michael Wyman had worked full-time at the College, he had usually found a convenient illness or distressed relative to prevent him from turning up. A few dons, however, enjoyed these sessions. The meetings provided an excellent forum for power games, outlandish proposals and verbal flatulence. Many dons had built their careers on such dubious foundations, and Council meetings were therefore entirely to their taste.

Council meetings were divided into two agendas.

First came the Open Business, where the College Fellows discussed the more mundane aspects of College affairs, such as student matters, complaints about the food and arrangements over social functions. Two undergraduates were present to represent the interests of the Junior Combination Room, the College's student union.

After the Open Business came the Reserved Business. The undergraduates would leave the room, and the dons could get on with the serious business of stabbing backs and wrangling over the College finances. Everyone was therefore anxious to end the Open Business as swiftly as possible.

"I believe that the Bursar would like to give us his proposals about the heating costs," said the Master.

"Yes," said the Bursar. He was an emaciated man with half-moon spectacles and impetigo, but despite this he had great dignity.

"In view of the ever-rising cost of fuel, I feel we have no option but to raise the heating charge on next term's undergraduate bills. I propose that we increase the cost by fifteen per cent."

"Thank you," said the Master. "Do any of the Fellows have any comment to make about this proposal?"

There was silence.

"Splendid. I assume we are all agreed, then. Perhaps the undergraduates present might have something to say."

He looked grimly down at the two students. They nodded humbly, and one jabbed the other with his elbow.

"Yes," said the prodded student. "Er—well, I'm not

sure if the—er—undergraduates will altogether approve of this—um—idea."

"Really?" said the Master drily. "Why not?"

"Well," stammered the student, "as you probably know, the student grants are only—er—going up by six per cent this year, so—well—it seems a little, um, unfair to put up heating by fifteen."

"Unfair?" boomed the Master indignantly. "Unfair?"

"Well, unfortunate, to say the least. I mean, as we understand it—and we could be wrong, of course—the national cost of fuel is only going up by five per cent, so—well—it seems a little, um, drastic to, you know, put up the College bill by fifteen."

"Perhaps the Bursar would care to reply," the Master said.

"Yes," said the Bursar. "I understand the students' feelings in this matter, but they must appreciate that we are in an economic recession. Even this College is not invulnerable to economic pressures. As Bursar, I must see things from a slightly broader angle than that of the students." He paused to let the other dons laugh politely at his little jest. "And so my proposals reflect this viewpoint. However, I have taken the student grant rise into account, and this is why I have only proposed an increase of fifteen per cent. The undergraduates should consider themselves fortunate that the increase was not substantially greater."

"Thank you, Bursar," said the Master. "I trust that answers the points you have made?"

He glowered ferociously at the undergraduates, defying them to pursue their complaint. They did not.

"Yes," said the undergraduates. "Thank you."

They did not look grateful.

"You may inform the JCR of the Bursar's magnanimity in this matter," said the Master. "Very well, gentlemen; that ends the Open Business. The undergraduate representatives may leave."

After the students had gone, the dons relaxed and settled back in their chairs, as if a bad smell had just been flushed from the atmosphere.

"I fear," said the Master, "that the Reserved agenda will take some time to complete. The main item concerns the College's financial crisis, and proposals for dealing with it. These are outlined in the notes accompanying the agenda, and I trust that we have all read them. Perhaps the Bursar would care to elaborate."

"Thank you," said the Bursar. "As we all know, the Government has directed the Department of Education to prune our support grant by twelve per cent. I need not spell out the difficulty this constitutes for the College."

The other dons coughed and nodded in assent.

"Therefore," continued the Bursar, "we have no choice but to explore all possible means of reducing College expenditure to compensate for this loss of income.

"Many of the suggestions I have outlined should meet with little dissent. Some, however, are more controversial. I would like to tackle these first, and to gauge the feelings of the Council towards them. I draw your attention to proposal 1(b): the termination of Honorary Fellowships."

There was a rustle of paper as the dons turned to proposal 1(b).

"Excuse me," croaked an aged archaeologist. "I seem to have mislaid the relevant sheet of paper. Does anyone have a spare copy?"

The Master gave the old don an impatient scowl, and he passed a copy down to him.

"Thank you so much."

The Bursar resumed his speech:

"As you all know, Honorary Fellows have special status in this College. Whereas other colleges merely give their Honorary Fellows free access to college libraries and invitations to formal dinners, we also bestow other favours. For example, our Honorary Fellows have full dining rights, unrestricted use of all College facilities, and the opportunity to teach and research if they so wish. Most importantly, they also receive a statutory pension.

"My basic proposal is this: Honorary Fellowships are a luxury which this College can no longer afford to bestow. Furthermore, we are not in a position to afford the Honorary Fellows we already have. Hence, I suggest that the special privileges held by Honorary Fellows be rescinded, and that their status be reduced to that of Honorary Fellows in other colleges."

There was a rumble of disquiet throughout the Council. The Senior Tutor raised his finger for attention. He was a grave little man who looked like a High Church vicar minus the dog-collar. He spoke in a sombre, fruity voice:

"Are we all aware that these Fellowships were established in 1576? This College is famed throughout the academic world for the privileges accorded to Honorary Fellows. We are the only College that does not bestow them upon cheap novelists, retarded royalty and Labour politicians, and our prestige is enhanced as a result. I fear that more is at stake here than the Bursar supposes."

The Bursar smiled unctuously.

"I am more than sensitive to College tradition," he said. "But I fear that this is one tradition that is no longer within our means."

"The Bursar's got a point," said an Australian mathematician. "Besides, who are these Honorary Fellows? A lot of them work elsewhere and get paid by other universities. Shouldn't they be getting this sort of recognition from their own places?"

This drew a murmur of assent from many dons.

"I suppose we had better examine a few individual cases," said the Master, "however distasteful that may seem."

"Yes," said the Bursar. "I have prepared the list. Firstly, let us look at Dr Michael Wyman. He is, I believe, a philosopher specializing in—" he consulted his paper "—philosophical logic. As I understand it, he has taught here for a total of nine terms in nearly thirty years. He works principally for the Foreign Office, and his Honorary Fellowship entitles him to return here whenever he retires from that job. He will also receive a full pension from this College."

"What precisely does Wyman do for the Government?" somebody asked.

The Bursar replied hesitantly:

"He is involved in security work of a highly sensitive nature. I think we had better concentrate upon Wyman the philosopher, rather than Wyman the civil servant."

"Perhaps," said the Master, "Dr Locke would care to tell us about Dr Wyman's professional standing."

Attention was turned to Dr Locke, the Director of Studies in Philosophy. He was an arid gentleman who struggled to overcome middle age with the aid of a low-quality hair dye. His face, perched above a paisley bow tie, had the colour and texture of a walnut. When he concentrated, his expression would fold into a variety of agonized contortions, as if he were permanently strapped to Torquemada's rack.

"Indeed," he said, "Michael Wyman's academic career has been somewhat...unfortunate. He was easily the most brilliant undergraduate of his year, and he promised to be an outstanding logician. Unfortunately, he developed a passionate interest in modal logic."

He paused.

"Why was that unfortunate?" asked the Master, half regretting the question.

"Because that was the area he chose to cover for his Ph.D. thesis. Two months after the thesis was completed, in 1953, W. V. Quine, the Harvard philosopher, published a book entitled *From a Logical Point of View*. This book did much to discredit assumptions popularly held at the time. One paper in that book, entitled 'Reference and Modality', effectively demolished the entire foundation of Wyman's thesis. There were many other casualties, of course, but Wyman was probably the youngest. Quine's essay destroyed Wyman's morale, and he was too immature to recover from the blow."

"I see," said the Master.

Locke nodded, and ground his dentures in further concentration.

"Yes," he said. "Wyman carried on working, of course, but he never regained his former zeal. He was quite a good teacher, I think, and his lectures were highly spoken of. The impetus, however, was gone. Then in '54—or was it '55?—late '54, I think, Wyman was recruited by one of the intelligence bodies.

"The College came to an arrangement with some Government department. Wyman was to be given the status of an Honorary Fellow, and he would return here when he became bored with playing James Bond. I don't know much else about the arrangement.

"Wyman has returned here occasionally, and he has done a spot of research and teaching. He has produced two papers: one was a reply to somebody's theory of reference in *Mind*, and the other was entitled 'Notes on Necessity'. They were adequate."

"Does anyone here know the precise details of the arrangements concerning Wyman?" asked the Master. "Apart from his Honorary Fellowship, I mean."

"I believe," said the Senior Tutor, "that given the peculiar circumstances of Wyman's departure, there is as little documentation on the subject as possible."

"Surely that is to our advantage," said the Bursar triumphantly. "Our commitment to Wyman is minimal."

But Wyman did not remain undefended. Help came in the form of Dr Arthur Hume, a wizened old English don who lived inside a dense cloud of pipe-smoke.

"The arrangement is not wholly without precedent," he said. "There was a Dr Austin who was employed by Military Intelligence. It was understood that the Foreign Office would provide us with some financial compensation, which would cover his subsequent return to the College.

"Unfortunately, Austin died in rather mysterious circumstances, so the arrangement was never concluded. Does not something of the sort apply to Dr Wyman?"

"I know of no records showing compensation for Wyman's departure," said the Bursar.

"There were no such records for Austin," Hume said. "It was a gentleman's agreement between us and the Government."

"That proves nothing," snapped the Bursar.

"The Bursar has a point here," said the Master. "And it does not seem to me that the Government has behaved towards us in a gentlemanly fashion lately."

"Exactly," said the Bursar. "We are continually reminded by the Government that circumstances are not what they were thirty years ago. The same argument should therefore apply in Wyman's case."

Hume frowned and tapped his pipe against an ashtray.

"I think you will find," he said, "that Wyman is not eligible for a pension from his present employers. He is expecting to receive one from this College. If we deny him it, we will be acting dishonourably, irrespective of whether or not we are under a contractual obligation."

There was another murmur of disquiet among the dons.

"Those are strong words," said the Master. "I do not feel there are grounds for calling the Bursar's proposals dishonourable."

"I can think of no other word to describe such proposals," said Dr Hume, "if they mean leaving a Fellow of this College without a pension or any recognition of his work."

"Since the bulk of Wyman's work has been for the Government," said the Bursar, "it is they who should recognize his efforts and achievements, such as they are."

"If Wyman had retained his full Fellowship, we would not be arguing about him now," Dr Hume said. "An ordinary Fellow has life tenure, and his position is assured. Wyman only exchanged his Fellowship for an Honorary Fellowship because it was an administrative convenience from our point of view. Had he known that everything could be sacrificed by making this move, he would never have agreed to make it. He will have every right to feel cheated and, I repeat, we will have acted dishonourably."

"Nevertheless," said the Master, "I am inclined to agree with the Bursar. Whatever arrangements were made concerning Wyman would have been an act of goodwill between us and the Foreign Office. Since all goodwill towards us seems to have vanished in the Government, I feel we are entitled—and in this case, obliged—to adopt a similar attitude ourselves. Does anyone have any other views to offer?"

There was a hint of defiance in his question, and the dons knew better than to challenge it. It would have been like trying to play on after checkmate had been called.

"In that case," said the Master, "I presume the Bursar would like a vote on his proposal."

CHAPTER FOUR

FEIGL'S CELLAR BAR LAY on the outskirts of the East German city of Erfurt. It was not the sort of place frequented by nice ordinary people who wanted a quiet drink in comfortable surroundings. On the rare occasions when nice people turned up at Feigl's they usually left after their first drink.

There were unpleasant rumours about the sort of people who frequented Feigl's. Most of them were true. Like every town, Erfurt has its pimps and racketeers, and Herr Feigl seemed to know what kind of beer they liked. After a hard day's criminal work, Erfurt's villains liked nothing better than a *mass* of lager and a game of cards in the cellar bar. The evening of May 5 was no exception.

By half past nine most of the tables in the bar were taken, and the air stank of tobacco fumes and alcohol.

Five separate card games were in progress: each of them provided a forum for various transactions and complex negotiations. The card-players growled, cackled and cursed as bottles tinkled, coins clattered and plans were laid.

At 10 P.M. Josef Grünbaum walked in. He was a large, burly man in his middle fifties. If every face tells a story, Grünbaum's ran to twenty volumes. It was scarred and leathery, chiselled into shape by a lifetime of cynicism and violence. Somewhere beneath his Neanderthal eyebrows, two little red eyes stared at the barman.

"A beer, Herr Grünbaum?"

"Yes."

One of the card players noticed Grünbaum's arrival and there was a chorus of greetings.

"Evening, gentlemen," said Grünbaum. His voice was slightly slurred, indicating a few beers elsewhere.

"What have you got for us, Josef?" asked a man at the back.

"Four thousand ballpoint pens, for starters. Any takers?" There was a murmur of interest.

"How much?"

"Two thousand marks the lot."

There was a pause as the drinkers considered the offer. "What else have you got?"

"I know where to pick up some fruit. Bananas, oranges. Maybe a few lemons."

"Where?"

Grünbaum grinned smugly.

"That would be telling, wouldn't it?" he said. "If anyone's interested, I'll work out a price. Think about it, gentlemen."

East German black-marketeers thrive on the sort of goods that Grünbaum had for sale. Even such mundane items as Biros are a scarce commodity in the DDR. Grünbaum had the knack of obtaining anything from carcasses of meat to boxes of sewing needles. He boasted that he could get anything, provided the money was right, and his clients were seldom disappointed.

Grünbaum succeeded because, unlike most of his competitors, he knew how to handle officialdom. His skill in the use of bribery meant that most of his activities were unimpeded by the police, and even though he was one of the most notorious operators in Erfurt, he had never been arrested.

This is not to say that Grünbaum was without enemies; there were a number of other racketeers who would have been quite happy to send Grünbaum to the bottom of the river Gera with a pair of concrete leg-warmers. Also, there was the ubiquitous Captain Mach of the *Volkspolizei*, the "People's Police", who had formed a deep-seated hatred for Grünbaum. This hatred was fuelled by Mach's awareness that most of his superiors were in Grünbaum's pocket, and that any charges laid against the black-marketeer would almost certainly be dropped.

Grünbaum liked his role as a disreputable Mr Fixit, and he played on it to the full. He boasted that his "friends in the Party" could supply him with anything from false visas to secret information. He even hinted at dealings with "friends abroad", though most of Grünbaum's associates regarded this as the rhetoric of an inflamed ego. Others were not so sure.

A voice piped up at one of the tables.

"I'll take the ballpoints off you, Grünbaum."

Grünbaum shook his head.

"No you won't. Not until you've paid me for those shoes. Six hundred marks, Frege, remember?"

"You'll get your money," said Frege.

"I certainly will," Grünbaum said. "You've got until the end of the week."

"You never said anything about a time limit," Frege said angrily.

"If you can afford to buy the pens, you can afford to clear your debts."

"That's a dirty trick, Grünbaum," Frege shouted. "You said I could take my time—"

"You've taken it. Now I'd like my money."

"You're a fucking Jew, Grünbaum!" Frege yelled. "A miserable, fucking Yid."

The other drinkers fell silent. Grünbaum's eyebrows knotted together in a frown.

"You'd better watch your tongue, Frege," he said. "I won't hear that sort of talk from anyone. Even from a young idiot who can't hold his beer."

Frege got up from his table. He was a large man, even bigger than Grünbaum. Despite his size and an advantage of twenty years' youth, most of those present did not highly rate his chances against Grünbaum. The older man was immensely strong, and although much of him had turned to flab, he could still put his fist through a door if he felt so inclined.

"Fucking Yid," repeated Frege. "All that bullshit about your connections and what a big man you are, but you still have to scrape the pfennigs out of the gutter to pay for your beer. You're just a fucking Jew, that's what—"

He was interrupted by the arrival of Grünbaum's fist on his jaw. The blow sent him spinning back, and he hit the floorboards with a crash.

"Now shut up and go home," Grünbaum said.

The drinkers laughed and watched Frege get to his feet. The expression on Frege's face indicated that Frege did not feel like going home.

"Who the fuck do you think you are?" Frege demanded. "You think you own this place, don't you?"

He picked up a chair and hurled it at Grünbaum. Grünbaum swept it aside with his right arm as Frege's left fist ploughed into his nostrils. Grünbaum replied with an upper cut that glanced past Frege's ear, and he felt a sharp pain in his solar plexus as Frege's right found another target. He lurched forward and smacked his head into Frege's face.

The customers at Feigl's bar found the brawl highly entertaining. Herr Feigl himself came out to watch the fun, but he made no attempt to stop it. He knew that Grünbaum would be more than willing to pay for the damage.

For about four minutes the two fighters seemed to be evenly matched. Most of the punches were landing, and the floor was awash with blood. Finally, Grünbaum managed to catch Frege off balance, and he sent him to the floor with a decisive right hook. The other drinkers gave Grünbaum a congratulatory cheer, and he replied with a twisted, swollen grin.

Just as Grünbaum was wiping the blood off his face, the door burst open and Captain Mach walked in with three armed vopos. Mach looked down at the concussed Frege, and then smiled triumphantly at Grünbaum.

"I might have known," said Mach. "Drunken and brawling. I'm ashamed of you, Grünbaum."

"Piss off, Mach," said Grünbaum elegantly. "You aren't needed here."

"Oh yes I am. You've just beaten up our friend Frege."

"Crap," said Grünbaum. "We both slipped on the floor. Didn't we, Frege?"

Frege moaned. The drinkers burst out laughing.

"They could hear you both slipping at the other end of the street, Grünbaum. It's not good enough, I'm afraid. You're under arrest."

"What?" Grünbaum stared at Mach incredulously. "You can't just—"

"Oh yes I can," smiled Mach.

"This is harassment," said Grünbaum. "You can't make any charge stick, and you know it."

"I'll decide that. Sergeant, put the cuffs on Herr Grünbaum."

"The first man who comes near me will get his balls torn off," Grünbaum said.

"Don't be an even bigger imbecile than you already are," urged Mach.

"I mean it, Mach. You've no right to arrest me."

"Haven't I just?" Mach said. "Brawling isn't the only thing we've got on you, you know."

"What are you talking about?"

"Think about it, Grünbaum."

Grünbaum paused and looked straight at Captain Mach's smiling face.

"You're bullshitting," he said.

"Come to the station and find out."

"Come and get me."

Mach sighed.

"If you insist," he said. "Sergeant..."

The sergeant ran forward and then ducked to avoid Grünbaum's flying beer glass. Mach moved forward with another policeman, and Grünbaum picked up another glass. A shot rang out and the glass smashed on the floor. Grünbaum gave a little gasp and collapsed.

Mach turned and saw one of the sergeants holding a smoking pistol. The sergeant paled and lowered the gun.

"He was going to..."

"It's all right, sergeant," Mach said. "Just call an ambulance."

CHAPTER FIVE

THE SETTING SUN TINTED the sandstone College buildings a deep sienna. Doctors Wyman and Hume ambled gently past the iron gates of a fifteenth-century courtyard and into the Fellows' Garden. Spring had touched the Garden, casting it into a riot of flower and blossom.

"So there's to be no reprieve," Wyman said.

"No, I'm afraid not," Hume said.

"Were you the only one who spoke on my behalf?"

Hume nodded sadly.

"It had all been decided in advance, I'm sure of it. The Senior Tutor gave a grumble of dissatisfaction at first, but he joined the Bursar when he saw which way the wind was blowing."

"And what of Locke? Didn't he say anything?"

"He was all for it, I'm afraid."

"But..." Wyman faltered. "Locke, of all people. For God's sake, Arthur, Locke knows better than anybody that I can do my job. Why...?"

"It's not just you, Michael," said Hume. "All the Honorary Fellowships are being rescinded."

"They could give me an ordinary Fellowship if they wanted to. Surely that would solve the problem."

Hume shook his head.

"No, Michael. Locke talked about your Ph.D. and Quine, and all the rest of it. They decided that you're a has-been."

"That was thirty years ago. Thirty years! I was a child, Arthur, an infant!"

They sat on a bench and watched the sun fade behind the College chapel.

"Perhaps if I spoke to the Master..." began Wyman.

"If you saw him now," said Hume, "the results would be wholly predictable. He'd sit you down with a glass of sherry, talk over old times, and show you to the door. You'd achieve nothing."

"I see." Wyman sighed and lit a cigarette. "I was looking forward to coming back. It wasn't the salary, or the pension, or anything like that. I just thought I would be coming home."

Hume smiled sadly at his friend.

"I'm sorry," he said. "Truly."

CHAPTER SIX

"**F**IVE ACROSS. A PLACE that sells Spanish wine. Six letters."

Wyman squinted at the ceiling.

"Spanish wine," he repeated. "Mmmm."

He looked down at the crossword. Six down read: *Metaphysical poet put on in close-up*. He entered the word "Donne". Seven down was *Take a busman's holiday as an actor (2,2,4)*, which must be "Go on tour". That meant that five across must be "Bodega". Things were proceeding nicely.

It was the morning after Wyman's last visit to the College. He had not slept well that night and did not feel inclined to work. Like many people whose world has been suddenly dismantled, Wyman was coping by immersing himself in trivial distractions. The *Daily Telegraph* crossword was ideally suited to this purpose.

"Eight across: *Absorbing business offer (4,4,3)."*

Wyman entered the words "Take-over bid" and took a sip of his coffee. His in-tray contained a large pile of documents, including half a dozen East German newspapers. These newspapers were seldom informative, but reading them was part of Wyman's weekly chores. He looked at them in distaste and lit a cigarette.

"A master craftsman who misses out on his reading."

He inhaled a deep puff of smoke, exhaled it, and wrote "Skipper" under two down. He wondered if there was money to be made from compiling crosswords. At this stage, he reflected, he must consider anything. Both his employers had now dismissed him, and if the only way he could earn a living was to be by writing enigmatic statements like *A fruit drink very quietly brought in,* then so it would have to be.

Ten across was "apple". He wrote down this solution and picked up the first newspaper from his in-tray. It was the *Berliner Zeitung am Abend,* one of the DDR's national dailies. He leafed through it casually, pausing only to glance at an item about the opening of a new electricity station in Leipzig. Having done his duty, Wyman scrawled his signature on the top of the front page to indicate that he had read the paper. He then put it in his out-tray. Fourteen across, he noted, was *American fuel product of practical value.* This could be a tricky one.

The DDR has a number of different national newspapers, although they all contain the same news and opinions. This reflects the peculiar nature of East German politics. East Germany calls itself the German Democratic Republic, and it is proud that since its creation it has always housed several supposedly independent political parties. In theory, each party is represented by its own newspaper. In fact, because most of the smaller parties in the DDR are directly controlled by the Socialist Unity Party of Germany, the SED, all the newspapers say the same thing. The only differences are those of style.

The DDR's national newspapers seldom talk about any of the country's economic or social problems. Crime, food shortages and environmental problems are never discussed. Only the provincial newspapers mention such issues, which is probably why their export to the West is forbidden by the East German government. Hence, national newspapers were of little use to Wyman, since all that he was interested in would be found in the provincials.

Not that the provincials especially interested him either. Whatever one's feelings are on the ethics of state-controlled publications, it is fairly clear that the results in East Germany are excruciatingly dull. Wyman could only derive amusement from the pathetic efforts of the East German journalists to endear themselves to their political masters.

His favourite example came from the August 1980 issue of the dog-lovers' magazine, *Der Hund*. In most countries, dog breeding is not a political occupation. East Germany is an exception. *Der Hund's* editorial began as follows: "The decisions of the IX *Parteitag* of the SED… are the guide of conduct for all our members…" Wyman had pinned this remarkable leader column to his wall.

"Twenty-three across: *One badly treated, but given a repeat performance.*"

Wyman ran his pen through what little hair remained on his head and released a small cloud of dandruff.

"Of course," he muttered, and wrote down "Iterated". He ground out his cigarette in the ashtray and pulled out another newspaper. This was the *Thüringer Neueste Nachrichten*, a provincial organ of the National Democratic Party.

Wyman read the first two pages and saw nothing of interest. He turned to page three and read the heading "Erfurt man dies after shooting incident". The piece ran as follows:

> On the night of May 5, Josef Grünbaum was shot by police in a café in Erfurt. Captain Georg Mach and three officers of the *Volkspolizei* tried to arrest Grünbaum, who precipitated a violent brawl in the café. During the brawl, one other man was seriously injured.
>
> When the police officers tried to arrest Grünbaum, he flew into a violent rage and began a vicious attack on Captain Mach. One of the other officers shot Grünbaum, who was taken to hospital, where he subsequently died of his wound.
>
> Captain Mach later said: "Grünbaum was a drunken, disreputable man. He was uncontrollably violent, and my officers defended me in the only practicable way…

Wyman cut out the article and reread it. Whether or not the story consisted of lies or half-truths, one thing was certain: Josef Grünbaum was dead. That was of great interest to Wyman because Grünbaum had run a small network of spies in Erfurt. The information that Grünbaum had collected was passed on to the British Secret Intelligence Service, and Wyman was Grünbaum's case officer.

Wyman was a vague, untidy person. He gave the impression of being obscure and confused, and he was famed for his absent-mindedness. Certain unkind members of the Firm had suggested that he was suffering from a touch of premature senility. Nothing could have been further from the truth. Wyman's memory was almost photographic, and his powers of reasoning and analysis were far better honed than most of his associates ever realized. The problem was that Wyman's faculties were seldom required by the dreary mechanical work he was given. There were very few occasions on which he was required to *think*, but this was one of them. And he thought hard.

He took off his glasses and screwed his eyes up tight in concentration. As he did so, he flicked back through a mental catalogue of dates, people and events. He reached for his pen, and began to scribble notes on his desk-pad. Within twenty minutes, three pages of scrawl adorned Wyman's desk.

He put his glasses back on and read through his notes. Having satisfied himself that nothing had been left out, he lit another cigarette and drank the cold dregs of his coffee.

All thoughts of his dismissal from the College, or Margaret's pregnancy, or even the *Daily Telegraph* crossword, had been banished. A new problem had arisen, and Wyman was totally immersed in it. He picked up his telephone and dialled an internal number that connected him with MI6 headquarters on London's South Bank.

"Hello, this is Wyman at the Department. Could you put me through to Newspaper Records please...yes, I'll wait...Hello, George? This is Michael at the Department...very well, thank you. And how are you keeping?...Splendid. I need something to be sent here as soon as possible, if you can manage it...Copies of a DDR paper, the *Thüringer Neueste Nachrichten* for all of last October, December and January...Yes, all of them. If you could give them to one of the messengers and tell him to bring them here at once, I'd be immensely grateful...That's marvellous. Thanks awfully, George...Yes, definitely. Cheerio."

Wyman put the telephone down and looked out of his window at the London sky. It was still bloody cold out there, he reflected, but at least it was sunny.

CHAPTER SEVEN

From: *Compendium of Anglo/US Intelligence Systems (Classified) 1972* page 47, Section 2.

INTELLIGENCE GROUPS: CATEGORY F

Such groups consist exclusively of Eastern bloc civilians recruited before 1958. Their primary function is to report the activities of military and civilian administrators in zones otherwise inaccessible to NATO scrutiny.

Type-F networks are more rigidly structured than networks in other categories: individual members of the network deal exclusively with the Group Leader; their identities are known only to him and the appropriate British or US department. (See p. 71, "Allocation of Network Parentage".)

Group Leaders of Category F networks communicate solely with their British or US case officers. They are funded and maintained solely by the parent department, and this department is responsible for collation and distribution of all material received. Any withdrawal of funds or equipment on behalf of the network will be designated by the network number, the code name of its Group Leader and the title of the parent department.

N.B. It is an integral feature of Category F networks that individual members do not know the identities of their colleagues. Should this situation fail to hold, the network concerned should be disbanded immediately.

CHAPTER EIGHT

THERE ARE MANY SOLUTIONS to the perennial problem of office tedium. Some people—usually those with active intellects—pass their time by solving crosswords, creating paper-clip chains, developing new designs of paper aeroplane and inventing various Heath-Robinson contraptions made of Sellotape, rulers and string. This was the approach Wyman favoured.

Other people choose to devote their creative energies to the enhancement of their job. For example, the true bureaucrat enjoys nothing better than inventing unsolicited "cost analyses", improving filing systems, and drawing up "efficiency studies" on multi-coloured graph paper. These activities are no less trivial and irrelevant than the achievements of the paper-clip engineers, but they give an illusion of efficiency and relevance to the orderly running of the office.

40

Owen, Wyman's chief, belonged to this second school of thought. Countless breakdowns, analyses and projections flowed from his pen. They were typed out, duplicated, circulated and thrown into waste-bins by those who received them. If Owen was aware of this, it did not bother him. The repeated Government demands for economies and reductions in spending merely charged his enthusiasm. He replied to every Ministerial memo on the subject with one more statistical salvo, confident that it would keep his masters happy.

Owen's background was military, as was his appearance. His neatly trimmed moustache and Brylcreemed hair adorned a stern, impassive mien that had taken him thirty years to perfect. He was concrete in every sense that Wyman was abstract. Although the two men shared many views, Wyman had reasoned them out, while Owen had swallowed them as blind dogma. They shared a world polluted by deception and brutality, but each had his own way of retreating from the stark realities of his job. Wyman turned facts into concepts, and took refuge in a sanctuary of abstractions; Owen built a stockade out of rule-books and Ministerial directives. Wyman's air of detachment found little favour with the Whitehall mandarins; Owen's blind submission was precisely what they wanted. Thus, Owen was assured of seniority and an index-linked pension, while Wyman was to be exiled into ignominy.

Intercourse between the two men was usually polite and arctic. When Wyman asked to see Owen about a matter of some urgency, Owen made a great point of looking at a blank page in his diary.

"You're in luck, Michael," Owen said. "I have no appointments this afternoon. Do take a seat."

"Thank you," Wyman said.

"What's the problem?"

"It may come to nothing, but there are some news items I collated recently. Taken individually, none of them is terribly significant. When seen together, however, they form a disturbing picture."

Owen picked up an HB pencil and began scraping the wax out of his ear.

Wyman went on: "The first is an item of news in an East German local paper. It reports the arrest of Otto Gödel for drunken behaviour in Erfurt on the night of October 21."

He passed a newspaper cutting to Owen.

"As well as this, we have a list of new arrivals at the Heisenberg Psychiatric Institute in Mühlhausen for the week ending January 4. You may recall that we decided to monitor the intake at that hospital because an unusually high number of political prisoners was being transferred there."

"Well?"

"On January 1 a Kurt Neumann was arrested and taken there on a specific charge. See?"

He passed the list to Owen.

"The last document is a public notice listing the names of certain people arrested and convicted of illegal trading in foreign currency. One of the names is Günther Reichenbach. He was arrested on December 18."

"Very interesting," Owen said. "Perhaps you'd care to explain."

"Certainly," Wyman said. "All these men were members of network ERF1O6F, headed by Josef Grünbaum, code-named 'Dovetail'. Dovetail was a small-time criminal who indulged in theft, pimping and black-market activities. His allegiance to us was strictly mercenary, though he was of some use. Whenever there were military exercises in Thuringia he was able to fill in the gaps in our knowledge. He also had some useful friends in the *Volkspolizei*, and he tipped us off about the first Brandt visit to Erfurt in '70. I was his case officer.

"Now to the meat of the story. Here is a copy of the *Thüringer Neueste Nachrichten*, dated May 6. This article here—" he tapped the paper—"completes the picture. Dovetail was shot while resisting arrest at the scene of a café brawl on the night of May 5. Taken to an army hospital, dead on arrival. Or so we are led to believe."

"Are you suggesting that Dovetail was blown?"

"Since they have been rounding up his network one by one, I can reach no other conclusion. And there lies the problem. Dovetail's set-up was an F-network: so how were the Germans able to arrest the members before the leader? You will note that all the arrests precede Dovetail's own. But that is supposed to be impossible; none of these people knew the identity of the other members of the network. So if they were arrested before Dovetail, the question arises…"

"Of how the Germans could have discovered the network?" Owen nodded thoughtfully. "Tricky one, that."

"Indeed," Wyman said. "You see, F-networks were established to avoid precisely this situation. The only people who knew the names of Dovetail's group were Dovetail himself and us. Assuming that Dovetail did not sabotage his own network…"

"Good God!" Owen exclaimed. It had dawned upon him at last. "Are you saying that we've got a leak in the Department?"

"No. I'm merely asking you for a better explanation. The only record of network ERF1O6F is kept in one file in this department. As with all F-networks, funding was channelled entirely through the leader, in this case Dovetail. The only entry on the central payroll is 'Dovetail', with the network number. All communication with the network was conducted exclusively with Dovetail himself.

"Therefore, there are only two ways in which ERF1O6F could have been exposed. The first is if Dovetail himself was discovered and made to reveal the identity of his accomplices. The second is if someone here passed on the details of ERF1O6F's personnel to the Germans."

"Good God," repeated Owen. "This is monstrous."

There was a pause as Wyman allowed Owen to register the full implications of his discovery. Wyman noted with quiet amusement a series of Ministerial memoranda on Owen's desk. They were all concerned with saving money. Wyman knew that within a day the same memoranda would be circulated throughout the Department under Owen's name.

"The Minister will have to be told," Owen said.

"Of course," Wyman said. "And he will want to know what we're going to do about it."

"Yes." Owen toyed nervously with his pencil. There were lingering traces of ear-wax on its point. "This is what every departmental head dreads, Wyman."

It occurred to Wyman that Owen must have viewed

this eventuality with particular trepidation, since the Ministry manuals had nothing to say on the subject.

"I have no choice but to put you in charge of the investigation," Owen said. "You must be thorough, but discreet."

"Naturally. I will need to travel to Europe to begin my inquiries."

"Why?" asked Owen suspiciously.

"I will need to find out the exact circumstances of these arrests. Ordinarily I would do so through the normal channels of the Firm. Since we wish to minimize publicity, I will have to avoid these channels and use a back door."

"What do you have in mind?"

"I'd prefer not to explain the details, if you don't mind, but suffice it to say that I do have some contacts throughout Europe who aren't working for anybody at the moment, and who might have access to the kind of information we need."

"I see," Owen said, though obviously he didn't see. "Is this all going to be very expensive?"

"I don't know," Wyman said flatly.

"We can't afford to finance holiday trips, you realize."

Wyman suddenly felt an overpowering urge to grab Owen by the throat and bang his head against the desk.

"I'll keep the expense to a minimum," he said.

"Do that," Owen said. "There's a recession on, you know."

CHAPTER NINE

WYMAN'S SON RICHARD LIVED in a squat in Hackney. He shared it with two girls and a fourth party of dubious gender called Leslie. Wyman did not know whether Leslie was a male homosexual or a female transvestite, and he was always too embarrassed to ask. So when Leslie opened the front door one afternoon, Wyman merely said:

"Good afternoon. Is Richard in?"

"Why hello, Dr Wyman," Leslie said. "Yes, he's upstairs. Do come in."

Wyman entered the hallway and noted that Leslie's hair was now a delicate shade of violet, which clashed with Leslie's orange eye-shadow and green lipstick.

"I presume he's still in bed," Wyman said. "After all, it's only three in the afternoon."

"He's a delicate boy," Leslie said. "He needs rest."

"He's always resting," Wyman said. "Perhaps one day someone will tell me what he's resting from."

"I'm sure you can guess," Leslie grinned, winking an eye.

Wyman shuddered and went upstairs.

Richard's door bore the legend "Abandon all hope ye who enter here". Wyman read it, smiled, and knocked.

"Richard? It's your father," Wyman said. "You know, the man who clears your overdrafts for you."

"Come in," Richard mumbled.

Wyman opened the door and beheld the cataclysm in Richard's room. Wyman was not a tidy or fastidious man, but he was positively spartan in comparison to his son.

"Hi, Dad," said Richard. He grinned sleepily from beneath a duvet, surrounded by an avalanche of books, records, dirty clothes, magazines, plates of decaying food, coffee cups, bottles and cigarette packets.

"Good afternoon," Wyman said. "I see that little has changed around here. You still wake up at the crack of sunset, your friends are still having hormonal crises, and you still have a splendid disregard for those old bourgeois concepts of order and hygiene."

"Spare me the irony," Richard groaned. "It's too early in the day. Have a seat."

Wyman waded through the rubble and found a chair that was relatively free of garbage. He sat down and offered his son a cigarette.

"Thanks," Richard said. "What's new?"

"A lot, actually. That's why I called." Wyman lit both their cigarettes, took a deep puff and continued.

"Firstly, the Firm is making me redundant, and secondly, so is the College."

"Wow!" exclaimed Richard. "What happened?"

"The Chancellor's last budget happened. You may recall that two areas were particularly badly affected by the reduction in spending: the ministries and higher education. I am the victim of both economies."

"Wow!" Richard repeated. "The Firm...well, I can just about understand that. But the College...I thought you were one of those immovable Honorary Fellows— life tenure, full pension, all that shit."

"I was."

"So what went wrong?"

"As part of its new economy drive, the College has decided to abolish Honorary Fellowships. The amendments to the College Statutes were voted through at the last meeting of College Council, and they gave us no leave to appeal."

"You mean the motion was streamrollered through the Council by the Bursar or someone like that."

"Almost certainly. Apparently there was little opposition to the idea within the Council—"

"And I suppose they didn't bother to ask the Honorary Fellows what *they* felt about the idea."

"Quite. The issue is settled, so in a few weeks' time I shall be entirely without work."

"That's bad," Richard said.

"The news didn't fill me with elation, I must confess. But that isn't all that's happened. The other news is about Margaret."

"How is she?"

"As a matter of fact, she's pregnant."

"Whaaat...?" Richard's eyes bulged with astonishment.

"You heard me. She's expecting a child."

"You're taking the piss," Richard said, shaking his head.

"I most certainly am not."

Richard threw back his head and laughed until tears ran down his face.

"I suppose...I suppose it was an accident," he gasped.

"Let's just say it came as a pleasant surprise."

"Are you sure it's yours?" Richard giggled.

"Of course I'm sure," Wyman snapped. "We don't all take a different partner each night, you know."

Richard howled with mirth and reached for a half bottle of Scotch that lay on the floor.

"This calls for a celebratory drink," he said, and took a long pull from the bottle. "Here, have a swig."

"Don't you bother with glasses or cups around here?" Wyman asked.

"They're either broken or filthy," Richard said. "Believe me, the bottle's safer."

Wyman shook his head in disgust and drank from the bottle.

"I don't believe it," Richard grinned. "I'm going to have a sibling. Or is she going to abort?"

"No, we will have the child."

"We?"

"Yes, we," Wyman said. "We intend to marry."

"Marry? Wow. This is more news than I can handle at one sitting. Well, congratulations. No one can accuse you of being predictable, can they?"

It was Wyman's turn to grin.

"It does all seem to have happened at once. It will be nice to have another child, but it won't be easy, given my redundancy."

"I bet."

"That's really why I've come to see you. I hope you appreciate that my financial position has changed dramatically. Quite simply, Richard, I won't be able to bail you out next time you get into trouble with your bank. The money just won't be there."

"I see," Richard said.

"I hope you do see. I'm afraid you will just have to get used to the idea of working for money, distasteful as it may sound."

"It not only sounds distasteful, it is. But I'll manage."

"Most people do," observed Wyman. "Your mother always felt that I was wrong to reach for the chequebook whenever you needed money. She believed that I was subsidizing a slothful, unproductive existence, and she was probably right. I didn't mind very much, as long as the money was there, but now it isn't there any more. Whatever I have will be needed by Margaret and the child, and..."

"Don't worry," Richard said. "You don't need to make excuses. I've stung you for far too much already. Thanks."

"Don't mention it," Wyman said, a little embarrassed.

"How are you going to manage?"

"I'm not sure," Wyman said. "I've looked for academic posts, but it's all science and computers nowadays. There's little call for philosophical logic, and my field—modal logic—is well and truly in the hands of the

Americans. The big man is a fellow called Kripke, and judging by what I've read, his whole line of approach is entirely different from mine."

"What does all that mean?"

"It means that I'm out of touch, and I need a research fellowship in a reasonably tolerant faculty that will allow me to find my academic feet again. Outside my university, that's a very tall order. All I could get would be a fairly junior post in a redbrick somewhere, and I doubt if it would pay enough to live on."

"It sounds bad."

Wyman shrugged.

"We'll see. There's no point in being gloomy until all the possible avenues have been explored."

Richard lit a cigarette and frowned.

"What amazes me is that you don't sound at all angry or bitter about what they've done to you."

"They? Whom do you mean?"

"The people who sold you out. Your loyal masters in the Firm, and that bastion of traditional virtue, the College. Don't you feel really pissed off about them all?"

"Why should I?"

"Oh come on," Richard groaned. "You've always prided yourself on belonging to the Great British Establishment. All my life I've heard you witter on about what a great set-up it is. Now, after all you've done for them, they've kicked you out. Why don't you admit that they're all a bunch of back-stabbing, hypocritical bastards? So much for the old school tie, all for one, one for all, and all that crap."

"I'm an academic, Richard. Not a musketeer."

"You get my point," Richard said. "They've ripped

you off, and you won't see it. The joke is that you asked for it."

"What do you mean?"

"You're getting what millions of others have suffered before you, and you were quite prepared to vote for it as long as you weren't in the firing line. In a way, you deserve all this for voting Tory."

"And that piece of poetic justice makes everything all right, I suppose?"

"No, it doesn't. It's not that I don't sympathize, but—"

"But you find the whole thing rather satisfying. I thought you Socialists claimed to have the compassionate ideology."

"You know what I mean," Richard protested. "I just want you to admit that your great faith in the Establishment was misplaced. The whole justification for that exclusive little club is that it sticks together and leads the rest of the country up out of the slime. Truth is they can't even take care of their own, let alone anybody else. You've spent a lifetime working for that system, and it's kicked you in the balls when you needed it most. Why can't you accept that?"

Wyman stiffened and stared coldly at Richard.

"Now you listen," he said slowly. "The 'system' you abuse so casually was responsible for your upbringing and education. The only reason why you can afford to lie back and insult my loyalties and allegiances is because this particular member of the 'system' has financed your idleness for the last twenty-four years. Despite all your fashionable squalor, your inverted snobbery and your Socialist affectations, you are still no more than a gentleman of leisure, which, I'm afraid, is a phenomenon typical of the British Establishment. My present circumstances in no way reflect badly upon the things I hold dear. Yours, unfortunately, do. The only criticism I can make of the 'system' you despise is that it's capable of producing intolerant ingrates such as yourself. Despite that, I'd be grateful if you showed a little more respect for my values, however eccentric they may appear to your enlightened mind."

There was a long embarrassed pause. Richard noticed that his father shook slightly.

"I'm sorry," he said. "I didn't realize…"

Wyman shook his head and lit another cigarette.

"I overreacted. The apologies should be mine. I'll have another drink, if I may."

"Sure."

Wyman took another swig from the bottle and grinned sheepishly at his son.

"I thought I was handling the situation calmly," he said. "But it's obviously hurt me more than I suspected. I admit I'm very confused at the moment. You…you touched a nerve, I'm afraid."

"I'm sorry."

Wyman waved his hand impatiently.

"Forget it," he said. "How's Cecilia?"

"Mum's fine. She asks after you."

"Give her my regards. And how's that fool she's living with?"

"He's fine too," Richard grinned.

"Never mind."

"Bitchy as ever."

"All dons are bitchy. It's their prerogative."

"I agree with the first half of that, but I'm not too sure about the second half. Anyway, you're not a don any more."

"No, I'm not. It will take getting used to."

"However distasteful the idea may sound," Richard smiled.

Wyman laughed and stood up.

"I'm afraid I have to go," he said. "I have a lot of unfinished work to clear up before I leave the Firm, so I probably shan't see you again for some time."

Richard nodded.

"Let me know when you're free," he said. "Perhaps we can meet for a drink—you, me and Margaret."

"That would be nice," Wyman said. "Goodbye, Richard."

"Thanks for coming. And…congratulations."

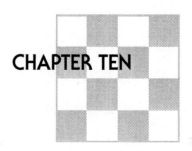

CHAPTER TEN

THE MINISTER'S CLUB IN PALL MALL served a class of men who were no longer supposed to exist. It was comfortable, oak-panelled, leather-furnished and very, very expensive. The same could be said of its members.

The Minister escorted Owen into the entrance hall and smiled benevolently at the hall porter.

"Good evening, Whitehead," said the Minister. "I believe the Russell Room is booked in my name this evening."

"Yes sir," said the porter. "The port's been put out for you. Will there be anything else, sir?"

"No, that will be fine, thank you."

The Minister walked regally up the circular stairs past faded paintings of past members. Owen followed him and noted that the club always smelled of cigars and brandy. When they arrived at the second floor, the

Minister opened a large door and led Owen into the Russell Room.

"Do sit down," said the Minister. He poured two glasses of dark, viscous port and handed one to Owen.

"Good health," said the Minister.

"Good health," Owen said.

They sank graciously into two leather armchairs.

"So," said the Minister. "You have something to tell me."

Owen explained Wyman's discovery, and its awful implications.

"Good grief," exclaimed the Minister. "This is ghastly."

"Monstrous. You agree that we must act?"

"Definitely. How dare they not decant the port!"

"I was speaking about Wyman," Owen said.

"Ah, yes. What are you doing about it?"

"I've had to put Wyman in charge, as you can appreciate. It is imperative that as few people hear of this as possible."

"Quite. However, it's all a bit embarrassing under the circumstances, what with Wyman being eased out and all that."

"I know," Owen said. "But that can't be helped. I must say, Wyman is being very sporting about the whole thing."

"Glad to hear it. The last thing we need is acrimony." The Minister poured out two more glasses from another decanter, and sipped his appreciatively.

"That's better," he said. "Damn good vintage, isn't it? So what is Wyman going to do?"

"He's going to Europe. Inquiries are going to have

to be pursued discreetly, so he's going to look up a few old contacts. Back-door inquiries."

"Yes," said the Minister suspiciously. "Sounds expensive."

Owen's moustache twitched with embarrassment.

"I know. But that can't be helped. Under the circumstances."

"Mmmm." The Minister frowned. "I really must get a case of this stuff for my home. Listen, Owen, I can't afford to subsidize Wyman's old-boy reunions if they don't bear fruit. That will have to be made clear to him."

"It has been," Owen said reassuringly.

"Thing is," the Minister said, "there are little goblins whispering impure suggestions into the PM's ear. One of them is that your place should be shut down."

"Shut down?" Owen looked horrified.

"Well, that isn't the term they're using. They're talking about merging you with another Division. It amounts to the same thing."

"That's terrible," choked Owen.

"I know. I'm defending you to the death, old boy. Rest assured of that. The problem is that my words count for less and less nowadays. It's the humidity situation in the Cabinet, you know."

"Humidity?"

"Yes. No one likes wets any more."

"Ah. Yes. I see."

"So," the Minister went on, "the case for your continued existence must be based upon your willingness to function on a much tighter budget. No more of these ridiculous expense accounts. Wyman's a bit of a *spender*, isn't he?"

He made it sound like an accusation of homosexuality.

"I'm afraid so," Owen confessed. "But he is good."

"More to the point, he's leaving. Just make sure he doesn't burn up too much cash before he goes. I really must ask where they get this port from. I can't get hold of anything this good."

"It is a very fine port," Owen agreed. "What happens if Wyman finds anything—an infiltrator I mean?"

"I'm not convinced that there is an infiltrator. But if there is—well, I thought you chaps knew how to handle that sort of thing. Surely, the problem consists simply of finding the blighter. Just keep it all discreet, will you? We can't afford another Bettaney fiasco."

"There seem to be a lot of things we can't afford," Owen observed.

"Too right," said the Minister. "There's a recession on, you know."

CHAPTER ELEVEN

BETWEEN HALF PAST SEVEN and nine o'clock on weekday mornings, East Croydon railway station is thronged by commuters. Trains run from there to two destinations in central London: Victoria and London Bridge.

The morning of May 10 was no exception. Among the plethora of stockbrokers, clerks, secretaries, accountants and civil servants stood a well-dressed man in his late thirties called Anatoli Bulgakov.

Bulgakov was short, good-looking and permanently cheerful. His geniality was matched by excellent manners and a fine sense of humour, and his warm, open laugh won over almost everyone who met him. Ostensibly, he worked at the British-Soviet Chamber of Commerce. In fact, he was a major in the *Komitet Gossudarstvennoi Bezopastnosti*, the KGB.

His peers regarded Bulgakov with mild suspicion. They mistrusted his fondness for Savile Row suits, Rolex watches and other trappings of Western decadence. Only Bulgakov's superiors knew better. Despite his relatively low rank, he had been given a free hand to do whatever he pleased throughout Europe: his freedom from bureaucratic restraint ensured the safety of countless operatives in his care. His record was one of unblemished excellence.

Bulgakov boarded the 9.05 train for Victoria and sat in the window seat of a second-class smoking compartment with his attaché case and a pocket romance entitled *Love's Revenge* by Bernadette Williams. Books like this baffled Bulgakov. He failed to see why the British working people should devote so much time and money to prose of this sort:

> Vera's heart throbbed in anguish as Milo held her in his passionate embrace. She felt his warm, sweet breath, and panic surged within her.
>
> "No, Milo," she breathed. "We mustn't. The Count will be here soon."
>
> "Hush," Milo whispered. "I will deal with Count Adolfo when he arrives."
>
> He kissed her tenderly and stared deep into her azure eyes. A tear rolled down her face, and he brushed it away with a gentle sweep of his finger.
>
> "We will never be parted," Milo said.

Bulgakov suppressed an urge to vomit all over the page, and he reflected that Marx's dictum on the opium of the people could be fruitfully applied to areas other than religion. Indeed, it was a mystery to Bulgakov how

Marx, who had written his great works in London, could ever have drawn inspiration from the British proletariat. Judging by the contents of *Love's Revenge*, the Anglo-Saxon workers had a long way to go.

He shut the book in disgust and put it beside him. The train rolled into Clapham Junction Station, and more passengers got on. A vast, wrinkled woman in an orange floral dress sat beside Bulgakov. She too had a copy of *Love's Revenge*. Unlike Bulgakov, she found the saga of Milo and Vera enthralling.

Bulgakov stared at the woman in horrified fascination. All his doubts about the English proletariat were summed up by this menopausal monstrosity. What would Marx have made of such a creature, with her blue-rinsed hair, butterfly spectacles and huge plastic earrings shaped to resemble bunches of grapes? Could the Revolution truly begin here?

Bulgakov forced himself to look away from the woman. He could face tortured suspects with equanimity, he was indifferent to the sight of demonstrators being shot, and the faces of arrested dissidents left him wholly unmoved, but this—this was too much. There were limits to what even a KGB officer should be expected to witness.

The woman continued to read *Love's Revenge* with avid interest. As the train entered Victoria Station she put the book down and dipped into her handbag for her ticket. Having found it, she shut the bag, picked up Bulgakov's copy of *Love's Revenge*, and got off the train.

Bulgakov watched her go, and noted that her stockings were full of holes, exposing tufts of hair and varicose veins. He shuddered and picked up her copy of

Love's Revenge. Stapled to the inside back cover were some folded documents. He put the book in his attaché case and left the train.

Inside Victoria Station is a branch of the National Westminster Bank. Bulgakov entered it, took £400 in cash from his attaché case, and paid the money into the account of Mrs J. Hobbes. He then left the station and hailed a taxi, which took him to the British-Soviet Chamber of Commerce, 2 Lowndes Street, SW1.

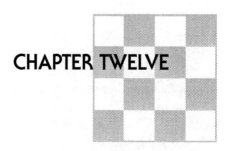

CHAPTER TWELVE

"**D**O COME IN," OWEN SAID. His tone was glacial.

Wyman closed the door and sat down in front of Owen's desk.

"How did it go?" he asked.

"The Minister was not pleased," Owen said solemnly.

"You know, I had a vague suspicion that he wouldn't be," Wyman smiled.

Owen gave a disdainful sniff.

"Like myself, the Minister is not entirely convinced by your conjectures."

"Indeed? Then how does he account for the fate of Dovetail and his network?"

"He doesn't. It is for us to explain these things."

"Quite," Wyman said. "So what exactly is going to be done about it?"

Owen looked downwards and toyed pensively with his moustache. He was one of those people who believe that long theatrical pauses can make the most mundane speeches sound impressive.

"The Minister has one overriding preoccupation. It is one I share. We are both concerned that this matter should not prove to be unduly expensive."

Wyman smiled cynically. "In medieval times there was a fashionable view to the effect that everything had a 'just price'. This notion seems to have been revived recently. What exactly is the just price of weeding out a Moscow infiltrator?"

Owen sighed wearily.

"Please don't be difficult. We are all under immense pressure with regard to money."

"So I've heard."

"My only concern is to keep the cost of this work to a minimum. There is no question of a 'just price'. We will pay whatever the job requires, within reason."

"Splendid," Wyman said. He suspected, however, that his idea of what was "within reason" would not correspond to Owen's.

"Hence," Owen said, "you may take a week's leave to pursue unofficial inquiries."

"A week?" said Wyman incredulously. "This could take months! What could I possibly achieve in a week?"

"You will at least be able to confirm your suspicions about the Dovetail network."

"They do not require confirmation. As far as I am concerned, we simply need to establish the identity of the KGB plant without delay. If I had a month, I think I could do it. In a week I could only begin my inquiries."

"Very well," said Owen. "Begin them. Your success or otherwise in the coming week will determine how we will proceed after that."

Wyman nodded. Clearly, Owen and the Minister were trying to persuade themselves that there was really no infiltrator in the Department. If Wyman returned with empty hands after a week, that would "prove" that his suspicions were unfounded.

"You said you would be making 'back-door inquiries'," Owen said. "But you weren't very specific about them. Perhaps you'd like to tell me now."

"I'd prefer not to. All I will say is that obviously we can't afford to tell this story to people who currently work for us or for the CIA. Hence, I will try to see what can be obtained from people who are no longer directly involved in intelligence work, but who still have some field contacts. I also have one or two personal connections who may be able to help."

"I see. Do impress upon these people the need for absolute secrecy. We can't—"

"I think they are quite capable of understanding the problem," Wyman said sardonically.

"Good. May I ask where you are proposing to make your inquiries?"

"I will need to go to Rome, Paris and Vienna. As I only have a week, I will have no option but to fly to these places, regrettable though the expense will be."

The irony in Wyman's voice had turned into mordant sarcasm. Owen, who was oblivious to sarcasm, gave a grunt of disapproval.

"Well, I suppose it can't be helped."

"I do not propose to keep in contact while I am

away. When I have returned you will be presented with a full report of my findings."

"Good," said Owen. He approved of written reports.

"I also have a request to make. I have now taken charge of all the documents relating to Grünbaum and his merry men. Before I leave I will lock everything in my office, and I would be grateful if the office remained locked until I return."

Owen gave Wyman an inquiring look.

"You are taking this very seriously, aren't you? Very well. I see no reason why you can't lock the office."

"Yes," Wyman said. "Unlike you and the Minister, I do spy strangers. And when I said I wanted the office locked, I meant that it should be permanently locked. No one should have access to it—not even the secretaries or Mrs Hobbes."

"I understand," Owen said curtly. "Is there anything else?"

"No, thank you," Wyman said. He got up and walked over to the door. Just before opening it he turned and smiled at Owen.

"Wouldn't it be amusing if I'd made one fatal error of judgment?" he asked.

"And what would that be?"

"The childish assumption that you yourself are above suspicion."

He laughed quietly as he left the room.

CHAPTER THIRTEEN

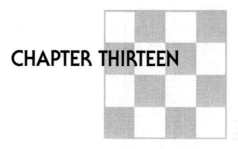

WYMAN FLEW TO ROME on the morning of May 11. He travelled under the assumed name of Edmund Ryle, using a false passport he had acquired when doing field work for the Firm. When its employees have finished their work abroad, the Firm insists on the immediate return of all their bogus documentation. However, Wyman had managed to delay the return of the Ryle passport until it had officially expired. He then applied to have the passport renewed, and upon receipt of the new passport he returned the old one to the Firm. Hence, unknown to his employers, Wyman was able to travel under an assumed name whenever he pleased. Given the nature of Wyman's trip, and his obvious desire that no one but himself and Owen should know what he was doing, keeping the false passport had turned out to be a good idea.

The flight from Heathrow Airport to Rome was brief and comfortable. Wyman sat in the first-class compartment of a British Airways TriStar, sipping brandy and smoking duty-free cigars. About halfway through the journey, the pilot pointed out that they were flying directly above the Alps. Wyman looked out and saw nothing but a thick carpet of cloud. He leaned back in his seat and wondered how Owen would react when presented with his expense account for the trip.

Gradually the weather brightened, and the pilot announced that they would soon be landing at Fiumicino airport. Wyman was reminded to put his watch forward by one hour, and was told that Italian customs would allow him to bring in 300 cigarettes, a bottle of wine and a bottle of spirits. Since all these items were cheaper in Rome than on the plane, Wyman ignored the offer.

Just under three hours had elapsed when the plane landed. Aeroporto Leonardo da Vinci, better known as Fiumicino, consists of two terminals about 18 miles from Rome, on the Tyrrhenian shore. The airport epitomizes the Italian flair for needless bureaucracy, inefficiency and confusion. As Wyman waited to collect his suitcase, he watched the scattered regiment of airport officials run about shouting, cursing, demanding and receiving entire forests of official documentation, annoying travellers and abusing porters.

With a skill born of bitter experience, Wyman managed to escape this confused mêlée with relative ease. He walked out of the airport into a warm sunny day and hailed a taxi. Forty minutes later he was in Rome.

Few cities can be summed up briefly, and Rome

defies all concise descriptions. Suffice it to say that Rome is a coffee-coloured city whose exquisite beauty stems from paradox and contradictions. It is both vibrant and sleepy, surging with life twenty-four hours a day, and calmed by indifference to time. It is wildly cosmopolitan and yet typically Italian. It is both tasteful and vulgar, noisy and gentle, elegant and gauche. On a glowing spring day its streets are filled by tourists clutching cameras, fawning shopkeepers who shortchange their customers, plump housewives and their shrill Catholic progeny, wrinkled old men reading newspapers in cafés, slim youths on motorbikes, bronzed workmen, bubbly young virgins, stern priests, nuns with moustaches, homicidal motorists, the pilgrimage to the Vatican, the smell of roasting coffee and pungent cigarettes, blasts of laughter, torrents of abuse, appeals to heaven, shrugs of the shoulder, fury, joy, love and total indifference.

Wyman had not been to Rome for eight years, and he was delighted to be back. He was driven through the centre of town and up to his hotel at the top of the Via Veneto.

Rome's hotels are graded deluxe, first, second and third class. Wyman chose to stay at the Hotel Flora, which is graded first class. Its slightly dated décor and excellent service appealed to his collegiate tastes, as did the view it enjoyed of the Villa Borghese, Rome's most famous park.

He was led up to a sumptuous double room, where he unpacked his suitcase and washed off the dust of two airports. He shaved, dressed and smoked a cigarette. At 6.15 he went downstairs, gave in his key, and walked out into the Via Veneto. He saw the Porta Pinciana, two squat sixth-century towers that lead into the Villa Borghese. Opposite him lay Harry's Bar, one of the favourite haunts of the American fraternity. When Wyman had been posted to Rome, Harry's was an excellent source of CIA gossip.

He walked down to the corner of the Via Ludovisi, and smiled with recognition as he saw the Café de Paris over to his right. He made his way past rich tourists, flower vendors and newsstands, down to the intersection with the Via Bissolati. He passed the large, bright Palazzo Margherita, now the United States Embassy, and watched the embassy staff float in and out of the American Library across the road.

After this the Via Veneto quietened down, and Wyman walked a little more swiftly past older hotels, travel agencies and cheaper cafés where low-budget tourists haggled with high-budget whores. Eventually he came to the end of the Via Veneto and into the Piazza Barberini. Two centuries ago the Piazza had been a marketplace. Now it contained a large hotel, a cinema and an underground station. The only clue to its history lay in the baroque Tritone fountain, which Bernini had chipped out in 1637.

Wyman turned down the Via Sistina and finally arrived at his destination, an unremarkable little street called the Via della Mercede. He stopped at Number 55, a tall grey building bearing a plaque which read "Stampa Estera in Italia", and went in.

The Stampa is Rome's foreign press centre. It had been given by Mussolini as a gift to the world's journalists. Ostensibly, this was a civilized, benevolent gesture on the part of a great statesman who had once been a journalist himself. In fact, Mussolini's intention had been to put all his rotten eggs in one basket, and the Stampa had been liberally seasoned with phone-taps and other listening devices.

After the war, the Stampa's importance as a press centre grew steadily, until its heyday in the 1960s, when it housed a bizarre collection of international scribes whose professionalism was matched only by their eccentricity.

In those days, Rome was the playground of the rich and famous, and no one was better qualified to report their antics to an incredulous world than the denizens of the Stampa. Hungry for copy, their editors drove these correspondents into the sort of workaholic frenzy that results in heavy drinking, failed marriages, fights, nervous breakdowns, and first-rate newspaper stories.

Presiding over all this mayhem was Frank Schofield, the grand old man of the Stampa. Schofield was a vast edifice of sardonic American lard, famed for his trenchant wit and ferocious drinking. He had corresponded from Rome since the 1930s, and had managed to survive over four decades' worth of social, political and journalistic lunacy. The turbulent 1960s had come and gone, but Schofield was still there, watching the world with cynical detachment.

Wyman had befriended Schofield when working as the Section V (Counter-Intelligence) officer at the MI6 Rome station. Unlike most of his colleagues, Wyman was a true cosmopolitan, and this had earned him Schofield's respect. Wyman had quickly realized that Schofield's caustic, boozy front masked an active, penetrating intellect, and that the two of them had a great deal in common. They shared a mordant sense of humour, as well as a taste for good food, drink and intelligent company. Both men were skilled professionals, and both preferred to hide the fact. Furthermore, they had more in common than was generally supposed. Schofield had been involved in US intelligence during the last world war and he maintained acquaintances in the "Company", the CIA.

Wyman entered the Stampa and saw Schofield's sixteen-stone frame leaning against the bar. There was no one else there, apart from a long-suffering barman who was already catering for the American's liquid requirements.

"Hello, Frank," Wyman said. "How are you?"

"About five drinks under par," said Schofield. "How about you? Still pushing paper in Percy Street?"

"That's right. But not for much longer, I'm afraid."

"Fired?"

"The English call it redundancy. It amounts to the same thing."

Schofield shook his head and emitted a low whistle.

"I heard they're economizing."

"Yes," Wyman said. "I've heard the same thing."

Schofield grinned.

"Drink?"

"Scotch please."

The barman poured out the drink and gave it to Wyman.

"Were you prepared for it?" Schofield asked.

"I have to confess that I wasn't. Cheers."

"Still," Schofield observed, "I suppose you can go back to your university now."

Wyman shook his head.

"No I can't. The College is taking similar steps. Very soon I shall be entirely without work."

"Nobody likes an old-timer, Mike. What are you going to do?"

"God knows. I haven't really had time to think about it. Something rather unexpected has cropped up in the Firm, and I'm supposed to sort it out before I leave. That's why I've come to see you."

"I didn't think you came here to exchange pleasant reminiscences. What can I do for you?"

"I'd prefer to talk about it elsewhere, if that's all right."

Schofield's eyebrows lifted inquiringly.

"Oh, it's like that, is it? Is there any money in this?"

"Only my expense account."

"That'll do. I presume we can talk over a quiet meal, thanks to the munificence of the Firm?"

"I don't see why not. It's the least they can do, isn't it?"

"Too damn right," Schofield growled. "I might be cheap, but I don't work for free."

"That," Wyman observed, "should be the motto on your coat of arms."

CHAPTER FOURTEEN

WYMAN AND SCHOFIELD LEFT the Stampa and walked down to the Via del Corso. The main streets were still full of people, so they turned off into a series of small lanes that led to the Piazza Navona.

"It's much quieter nowadays, Mike," Schofield said. "No more big parties, crazy film stars, all that crap. Rome still makes for good stories, but I think it's sobering up."

Wyman gave a sly grin.

"Are you talking about Rome or Frank Schofield?"

"Both, I guess. You know, I think I've become just another tourist attraction. People put me down on their itineraries, somewhere between Trajan's Column and the Trevi Fountain. I get all these weirdos from the States coming up and telling me how they've heard all about me. It's very disconcerting.

"The other day I got a visit from some girl who

works at the US Embassy. She had her speech all ready. 'Hello,' she said, 'I've heard all about you. I've always wanted to meet you.' Then she took a good look at me and she said, 'But Christ, you're so fuckin' old!'"

He exploded into laughter.

"You know," he continued, "when I die, I think they're going to stuff me and put me in the Vatican Museum. I can think of one or two editors who think that should have happened twenty years ago."

"Are you still writing?" Wyman asked.

"Officially, I'm retired. I still do an occasional feature for one or two American magazines, but my heart isn't in it any more."

"What happened?"

"Nothing really," Schofield sighed. "I guess I suddenly realized that I'm an old man. It's taken a lot of getting used to. Like Edith's death."

"I was very sorry to hear about that. She was a marvellous lady."

"She was a drunken old slut," said Schofield. "But she had her good points."

They finally came to the Via della Scrofa and went into Alfredo's restaurant. This is one of Rome's more expensive eating spots, made famous by its excellent food and clientele of international celebrities, whose yellowing photographs adorn Alfredo's walls. Wyman reflected that if a great deal of MI6 money was going to be spent, at least it wouldn't be wasted.

The two men began with an *antipasto* of melon and Parma ham. Next came a starter of *fettucine* in a delicate sauce of butter, ham and mushroom, helped on its way with a bottle of *Colli Albani*, a dry amber wine.

After this, Wyman ploughed into a large plate of *abbacchio*, roasted baby lamb, served with a salad of tender greens with an anchovy dressing. Schofield ordered *Pollo Alla Diavola* and *Carciofo Alla Romana* (artichoke sautéed with garlic and mint).

After coffee and a couple of shots of *Sambuca*, the conversation turned to the purpose of Wyman's visit.

"So Mike," Schofield said, "tell me the big secret. Why are you in Rome?"

Wyman lit a cigarette and leaned back in his chair. "How much do you remember about the network coding system?"

"A little," said Schofield, smirking. "More than I should ever have learned in the first place."

"Do you remember what F-networks were all about?"

"F-networks. Mmmm. Let me see..."

He paused for reflection and said:

"Yeah, I remember. What about it?"

"Recently, an F-network in the DDR was blown. Ordinarily, there'd be nothing to worry about. Such things happen all the time. But on this occasion there was cause for concern because several of the members were blown before the network leader was exposed."

"Jesus!" Schofield exclaimed. "That isn't supposed to happen."

"Draw your own conclusions, Frank."

Schofield paused once more and looked at Wyman in consternation.

"That's very hot shit, Mike."

"Precisely. Only three people know about this: myself, the Minister and Owen, my boss."

"Owen. Little guy, military type? I met him once. Isn't he a faggot?"

Wyman smiled.

"I've really no idea. Anyway, for obvious reasons, Owen wants it kept quiet until our inquiries have been completed. That's why he had to put me onto the case. As you can imagine, it's all very embarrassing for him, seeing that I'm to be made redundant. But he has no choice."

Schofield found the irony of this amusing.

"And you're the one that's getting fired? No offence, Mike, but doesn't it occur to you that the Firm is run by a bunch of incompetent jerks?"

"We do have an unorthodox way of dealing with things, it must be said.

"So how do I fit into all this?"

"I'm supposed to be making inquiries outside all the normal lines of communication. That doesn't give much scope, but it occurred to me that you might be able to contact someone in the Company and make a few discreet inquiries on my behalf."

"What sort of inquiries?"

"I want to know if they've heard about this story, and if they have, I'd like to see what they've managed to pick up. There's no need to mention that virtually the entire network was blown or that it was an F-network. The network was based in Erfurt, and the leader's name was Josef Grünbaum. Just say that Grünbaum was blown, and that you'd like to know how it happened."

Schofield frowned.

"I'm not sure about this, Mike. Most of the Company people I know left Rome several years ago. I don't know any of the new boys. Still, if you give me a couple of days, I might be able to find out something for you. Mind you, I'm not making any promises."

"I don't expect any," Wyman reassured him. "I was going to suggest that I get in touch with you again in about four days' time. How does that suit you?"

"Well, if I can't get anything by then, you might as well give up on me. Okay, four days it is."

"Splendid," Wyman beamed.

"Furthermore," Schofield said sternly, "if I actually find out who blew this Grünbaum fellow, I expect a free meal at the Savoy, courtesy of your friend Owen."

"I'll put it to him," Wyman said. "I'm sure he'd be delighted."

CHAPTER FIFTEEN

Hotel Flora
Via Veneto
Rome
May12

My dear Margaret,

I hope you are well. The weather here is infinitely more agreeable than in London, and I am having a splendid time. Although I am only here for a day or two, I have still found the opportunity to visit several old friends in the neighbourhood.

Did I ever tell you about Neville Tanner? I once helped out with his monograph on Aristotle's *Prior Analytics*, and we became firm friends. He's doing something or other at the British School, and we met for a drink this morning. He was most upset to hear about my removal from the College, and he says he will send a formal letter of protest to the Master. I doubt if it will do any good, but I thanked him for the gesture.

Rome is as relaxed and unhurried as ever. (I believe the modern term for it is "laid back".) I find it difficult to reconcile this mood with the hurried nature of my trip. Had it been possible, I would have liked to stay here for another week, but I doubt that our mutual friend in Percy Street would have approved.

I expect to be back in London by the evening of the 16th. Perhaps we could have dinner somewhere, if that would suit you. I know I have been somewhat diffident lately, but I think you can appreciate why. A great deal has happened very quickly, and I haven't adjusted to my circumstances as swiftly as I thought I would. I think I must be getting old. Please bear with me, and forgive the eccentricities of a disorientated don.

Love,
Michael.

CHAPTER SIXTEEN

ANATOLI BULGAKOV SAT IN HIS spacious office in Lowndes Street. Spread out across the desk before him were the documents that Mrs Hobbes had given him three days before.

Earlier that day Bulgakov had been told by his KGB colleagues that Michael Wyman had left for Rome. Some months earlier, Bulgakov had placed Wyman's flat under close observation, and the scrutiny now bore fruit. Wyman had been discreetly tailed as far as Heathrow Airport the previous morning.

It was now obvious to Bulgakov that something important had happened in the Department. He knew enough about Wyman to realize that an impromptu flight to Rome was not part of Wyman's routine work. He therefore had to make sense of the information given to him by Mrs Hobbes.

Exhibit A was a photocopy of the item in the *Thüringer Neueste Nachrichten* relating the death of Grünbaum. Beside it was a photocopy of a page from Owen's desk-pad. It contained a string of handwritten notes which Owen had taken down when Wyman related his findings. There was a series of dates and cryptic remarks: "Grünbaum 5/5, *but* Neumann 1/1, Reichenbach 18/12, Gödel 21/10—technically impossible"; "Fix emergency appt with Min."; "W. to establish full circs of G.'s death".

Mrs Hobbes had also photocopied the extract from the *Compendium of Anglo/US Intelligence Systems* which Wyman had taken with him to the meeting. Presumably, Mrs Hobbes had decided that this was enough for Bulgakov to establish what was going on.

Bulgakov lit a cigarette and reread the documents. He began to wonder if he should not report all this back to Moscow Centre. Most of his colleagues would have been expected automatically to pass this sort of information back to Dzerzhinsky Square, where their superiors would process it and decide what was to be done. It was only because Bulgakov was an especially trusted operative that he could even contemplate handling all this on his own.

Indeed, the KGB is famous for allowing its employees almost no personal initiative in matters outside the USSR. It has frequently been described as a dinosaur. Although it is by far the world's largest intelligence organization, its rigidity of structure and procedure invariably leads to bureaucratic clumsiness and delays which do not impede the agencies of lesser nations.

The KGB hierarchy is vast and complex. At the top of the tree sit the Chairman and his deputies. Below these gentlemen are the four Chief Directorates, which in turn control a large number of subsidiary departments. The First Chief Directorate, Bulgakov's employer, is responsible for all foreign operations. The others deal with internal security, political, religious and ethnic dissent, and the control of all the border guards in the Soviet Union.

Below the Chief Directorates are nine ordinary Directorates. These handle the armed forces, surveillance, communications intelligence, political bodyguards, technical support for the rest of the KGB, research, administration, service and personnel.

Finally, there are six Departments which deal with special investigations, collation of operational experience, state communications, "physical security", registry and archives, and finance.

The headquarters of this colossal organization are in a seven-storey, ochre-coloured rococo building at 2 Dzerzhinsky Square in Moscow, which before 1917 housed the All-Russian Insurance Company. Behind it sits the infamous Lubyanka prison.

A nine-storey extension was added to the building during the Second World War, but even that proved too small to meet the needs of the KGB. Further buildings went up elsewhere in Moscow to house the organization's ever-growing staff. There is now an extra block on the Kutuzovsky Prospekt, as well as an enormous administration building on the Machovaya Ulitza, and an even bigger half-moon-shaped building just off the Moscow Ring Road.

It was in these buildings that Bulgakov had received his basic training as a KGB officer, before he was sent out of Russia as a captain in the First Directorate. He disliked having dealings with Moscow Centre, since he resented any infringement of his personal autonomy. He knew that if he reported the present situation to Moscow, his superiors would infer his inability to handle it. Bulgakov's record in Europe was spotless and he wished to keep it that way. He therefore resolved to tell Moscow nothing for the time being.

He studied the extract from the *Compendium*. This document clearly implied that Grünbaum was in an F-network. The other names on Owen's notepad must have belonged to other members of this network. So why had Owen added the words "Technically impossible" to this list of names?

The number "5/5" after Grünbaum's name gave the date of his death, since the newspaper item claimed that Grünbaum had died on May 5. Hence, Bulgakov reasoned, the other people must have died on the dates written by their names—Neumann on January 1, Reichenbach on December 18 and Gödel on October 21. But this did not explain Owen's remark: why was all this "technically impossible"?

Bulgakov reread the extract from the *Compendium* and the answer finally hit him. Given the definition of F-networks, the only thing that was "technically impossible" was that the members of the network should be exposed before the network leader. The leader must have been Grünbaum, and therefore...

"Shit!" he exclaimed. It was all clear to him now. He leaned back in his chair and thought very hard. The rest of Owen's notes now made sense: "Fix emergency appt with Min." meant that Owen was reporting his department's discovery to the Minister in charge. "W. to establish full circs of G.'s death" indicated that Wyman had been sent out to discover precisely how Grunbaum's network had been blown.

It occurred to Bulgakov that he too must find out exactly what had happened in Erfurt. Unlike Wyman, however, he did not need to do so by covert means. He would merely have to interview the East Germans responsible for Grünbaum's case. He would then be in a position to establish how far Wyman's inquiries could possibly lead him.

He wrote a memo for one of his secretaries, asking her to book a return ticket to East Germany on his behalf. His diary revealed that he would be needed in London for another five days, so he decided to fly to the DDR on the 20th.

He added a postscript to the memo which ran as follows:

"Please notify the Erfurt division of the SSD of my plans, and request that they make all the necessary preparations for my stay. I will be in Erfurt for no more than four days. In that time I intend to investigate the case of one Josef Grünbaum, and I will expect all the appropriate documentation to be available to me. Stress that this is a matter of the utmost urgency, requiring the strictest observation of security procedures. Only the minimum number of people should be notified of my visit."

CHAPTER SEVENTEEN

WYMAN FLEW TO GENEVA on the afternoon of May 14. After a pleasant thirty-six hours in Paris, the flight had no appeal for him. He regarded the Swiss as a nation of insipid nonentities who deprive you of your money in four different languages. Wyman's visit therefore took no longer than the job required.

He took a taxi to the Banque Internationale Descartes, 53 Rue Pascal, and was shown into the manager's office. Monsieur Georges Piaget was an impeccably polite cadaver with a limp handshake and an antiseptic voice.

"Good afternoon, Mr Ryle," he said to Wyman. "What can we do for you?"

"A great deal, I hope," Wyman said. "I am acting on behalf of another party who wishes to open an account at this bank. The gentleman concerned is also not a

86

Swiss national, and for reasons of discretion he wishes the account to be numbered. For the time being he wants me to act on his behalf in the matter of depositing and withdrawing sums from the account."

"I see," Piaget said. "That should present no difficulties, Mr Ryle. Nevertheless, since neither you the contracting party, nor the beneficial owner of the account are Swiss nationals, a certain amount of documentation is required."

"I appreciate that," Wyman said.

"Splendid. You are probably aware of what is required, but I will go through it all in case of difficulty. To begin with, Mr Ryle, we need documentation of your own identity—your passport would suffice."

Wyman drew out the false passport and handed it to Piaget.

"Splendid," Piaget repeated, noting down the passport number. "We will also need several specimens of your signature, and details of your place of residence. And of course, we need to know certain details about the beneficial owner of the account."

"Yes," Wyman said. "I think you will find all you need here."

He produced a typewritten document and placed it on Piaget's desk.

"This," he explained, "gives the gentleman's full name, and his place and country of residence. There is also a letter of introduction from a reputable European bank. As you can see, it confirms the gentleman's address and certifies the specimens of his signature given below."

"Excellent," said Piaget.

He studied the documents carefully, and if any of it surprised him, his face did not show it.

"This is more than sufficient," he added. "There are one or two standard documents we must request you to sign, and I will introduce you to the official who will be responsible for this account. You will appreciate, of course, that once the agreements have been signed, we will require a period of forty-eight hours to complete our own formalities."

"Of course," Wyman said. Piaget was really saying that the bank would need two days to make its own private inquiries about the *bona fides* of the beneficial owner of the new account.

"As a matter of fact," Wyman said, "I expect this account to remain unused for a week or two yet."

"Indeed," Piaget said.

"Yes. We then expect a very large lump sum to be paid into the account, and we expect it to remain there for a minimum of eight months."

"I see," said Piaget. "What sort of figure should we expect to receive, if the question is not an indelicate one?"

"You will find it written on the back of the page giving details of my client."

Piaget glanced at the sheet and slowly looked up at Wyman. Years of experience had taught Piaget to avoid expressions of pure greed, but there was a remote hint of it in his voice.

"This is quite a sum," he said.

"It is," Wyman agreed. "But I am sure you are perfectly capable of dealing with it."

"Quite so," Piaget said. "Perhaps your client would

like us to manage his account for him. The Bank provides an excellent service—"

"The possibility has occurred to my client," Wyman said, "and we shall probably discuss it at a later date. For the time being I am simply interested in establishing the account."

"I entirely understand," said Piaget, picking up his telephone. "Perhaps I can introduce you to M. Barthes. He will be responsible for your client's account."

Three minutes later Wyman was shaking hands with a pinstriped suit inhabited by M. Barthes and M. Barthes' last dozen meals.

The three men sat down and the remainder of the formalities were completed. Wyman signed the standard Form A of the Swiss Bankers' Association, entitled "Declaration for Opening an Account or Depositing Securities". In doing so, Wyman was declaring that he, Edmund Ryle, was merely the contracting party, and that the beneficial owner was someone else.

He then signed the formal agreement establishing the account, giving the name of Ryle and that of the beneficial owner. Appended to the agreement was a long list of general conditions.

Finally, because Wyman was opening a numbered account, he had to sign yet another document which was ponderously entitled "Special Agreement Completing the Contract for Opening an Ordinary Account and Deposit". This was supposed to indemnify the bank against any risks arising from using a code-number instead of a name in the account. The code G2H-17-493 was entered on the agreement, and that was that.

It was explained to Wyman that deposits and withdrawals would be made exclusively by means of this number. Despite the elaborate secrecy of this procedure, Swiss banks still regard numbered accounts as more vulnerable than "ordinary" ones, and so further precautions are insisted upon.

Wyman was told that cash withdrawals could not be made over the counter. To release any sum of money, Wyman would have to see his account manager in person, and M. Barthes would withdraw the cash under his own signature. The lowly cashier was far too untrustworthy to be allowed to handle numbered accounts.

Once the formalities had been completed, M. Barthes left, and M. Piaget gave a cigar and a glass of brandy to his new client. He expressed his delight at being able to do business with an Englishman.

"The English are such gentlemen," he enthused.

"Yes," Wyman said. "Perhaps that's why they get foreigners to handle their money for them."

"Perhaps," said Piaget. "The English have the most... unfortunate banking system. Your desire for privacy in domestic and social affairs is most laudable. It is a pity that it does not extend to your commercial affairs."

"Indeed," Wyman said. "This is because the English obsession with privacy is outweighed by the English obsession with tax."

"Quite so," Piaget remarked sadly. "It is most unfortunate."

"Do you really think so?" Wyman asked.

Piaget's face creased into a frozen smile.

"Of course not," he said.

CHAPTER EIGHTEEN

EDGAR P. RAWLS STRAIGHTENED his knitted-wool necktie as he walked along the corridor to his boss's office. He knocked on a door marked "293: NAGEL". From behind the door came a noise that sounded like the belch of a laryngitic duck. The noise bore a vague resemblance to "Come in", so Rawls opened the door and went inside.

Rawls was forty-one years old, though like most CIA men he could have been anywhere between twenty-five and fifty. His jagged face had no laugh-lines on it. A pair of dead-blue eyes stared grimly at the world through his tinted spectacles, and his expression was one of sardonic indifference.

He had joined the CIA early in 1965, where he was employed in the Special Operations Division. In the following year he worked in Vietnam under William

Colby (who was later the Director of the CIA) in Colby's Provincial Reconnaissance Units programme. The PRU had been set up to infiltrate the Communist areas for the purposes of disruption, intimidation, interrogation, abduction, terror and murder. Rawls excelled in all these fields.

In 1967 Rawls became involved in Colby's "Phoenix" programme in South Vietnam. Essentially, the work consisted of remorseless elimination of Communist spies, assassins and terrorists. In its first thirty months of operation, the Phoenix programme cost the Vietcong over 20,000 casualties. Of these, at least 3,000 were directly attributable to Rawls.

After this, Rawls was transferred to the Western Hemisphere Division of the CIA's Clandestine Services section. From November 1970 he worked in Chile towards the overthrow of Salvador Allende Gossens, who led that country's first democratically elected Marxist government. Once again, Rawls did his job with surgical efficiency.

Between 1975 and late 1977, Rawls was transferred to the CIA's Directorate of Intelligence, and he worked as a liaison officer between the CIA and the US National Security Agency at the American Embassy in Bonn. He was involved in the exposure and capture of Lothar-Erwin Lutze and his wife, Renate, both of whom had worked in the West German Defence Ministry. During his inquiries, Rawls discovered that the Lutzes had passed on NATO's secret defence plans for West Germany to the KGB, along with a great deal of research data and top secret communications. Rawls gave the news to the BfV, West Germany's counter-intelligence agency, and the Lutzes were subsequently brought to trial.

Rawls' extraordinary career did not end there. Between 1977 and 1980 he continued in the CIA/NSA liaison, but this time he was based in the US Embassy in Moscow. By then, however, the KGB had amassed a large and disturbing file on Rawls, and it was decided that an agent of such alarming efficiency could be tolerated no longer. In September 1980 Rawls was expelled from Moscow, and he returned to CIA headquarters at Langley, Virginia.

Rawls had now become something of an embarrassment to his masters. Clearly he was one of their top field operatives, but his usefulness at home was another matter. He could no longer be placed in embassies abroad without exciting comment, and he was becoming too old for the kind of spectacular clandestine work in which he had once excelled.

He was therefore put into the tender care of Milton K. Nagel, the head of Anglo-US Intelligence Liaison. Nagel's official brief was to ensure the free flow of intelligence between the CIA, the NSA, MI5 and MI6. Unofficially, his job was simply to extract the intelligence that the UK preferred to hide from the US. To do this, Nagel exploited every goodwill mission made by American officials to Britain, and he tapped every British phone call that the NSA could unscramble.

Rawls did not like his boss. Nagel was a loud-mouthed slob who ate hamburgers instead of taking baths. Unlike Rawls, he had a coarse, resonant sense of humour, and he was entirely open about his contempt for "smart-assed prima donnas", of whom Rawls was one. He was short, fat and sweaty, and he disliked Rawls' penchant for vigorous efficiency.

"Good morning," he said, as Rawls closed the door. "Take a seat."

Nagel leaned back in his swivel-chair and put his feet on the desk, knowing that this would irritate Rawls.

"Got a job for you," he said.

Rawls nodded.

"Some two-bit hood by the name of Grünbaum got himself arrested and killed in the DDR. It seems that this boy ran a Brit-sponsored network over in Thuringia, or somewhere like that."

"So?"

"So people are asking questions about it."

"What people? What questions?"

"The Brits have put some guy named Wyman onto it. For some reason they're worried by Grünbaum's getting blown, and they want to know how it happened. Christ knows why they're so upset. This kind of thing goes on all the time, and nobody gets screwed up about it.

"Funny thing is, instead of making the routine inquiries, Wyman's been avoiding the Firm altogether. Six days ago he got in touch with Frank Schofield in Rome."

"Who?"

"Frank Schofield. Old-time Kansas newspaper hack. Did some work for us during the war, and after that he used to help us out from time to time. He's retired now, but he still knows a lot of the old crowd, so he's still a good vehicle for discreet inquiries into the Company. Or so Wyman thinks."

"What happened?"

Nagel gave a frog-like smile.

"Schofield got in touch with one or two people over here, hoping that everything would be nice and quiet. In fact, our people gave him virtually nothing, and then they told me what was happening. Wyman was taking a stupid risk asking Schofield for help. He should have known that we'd find out about it."

"Who is this Wyman? How come he knows Schofield?"

"Wyman is a typical English cocksucker. I think he's a professor of philosophy, or something like that. He's pretty amateur, even by Brit standards, and that's saying something. Anyway, he met up with Schofield in Rome in the mid-fifties when he worked at the British Station. They've been good buddies ever since."

"Okay," Rawls said. "So what do I do?"

"If Wyman is avoiding routine lines of inquiry, it means something funny is going on. If something funny is going on, I want to hear the joke. I mean, if you want to know why some op. has just got burned in Germany, you don't normally go running to some old fossil in Rome. If you want Company help, you ask the Company, right? So why doesn't Wyman want us to know what's going on? I want you to find out."

Rawls frowned.

"Sounds as if I might be chasing my own ass."

"Sure you might," Nagel said.

"Yeah."

Nagel grinned evilly.

"What's the matter, boy? You don't look too happy about it."

"That's because I'm not. I've got one old idiot in London, another old idiot in Rome, and some prick in Germany who doesn't know how to run a network properly. What kind of network was this, anyway?"

"Don't know," said Nagel. "You'll have to find out. We do know what kind of stuff he was sending back."

"Go on."

"This is an old network." Nagel referred to some notes. "It never produced a regular supply, but there's stuff been coming over since '57 that we know about, and it's probably even older than that.

"Most of the stuff's chicken-feed. Troop movements, stuff like that. There was only one moment of glory, back in '70. If you remember, Brandt met Stoph at Erfurt for the first time, and this guy Grünbaum got the word on it nice and early. That gave us time to act."

"Yeah," Rawls said. "I remember."

The occasion Nagel was referring to was the Erfurt meeting on March 19, 1970, between Willy Brandt, the West German Chancellor, and Willy Stoph, Chairman of the East German Council of Ministers.

It was the first official meeting between East and West Germany, and it resulted in diplomatic relations between the two nations. That in turn led to the four-power Berlin Agreement, which allowed full international recognition of the DDR.

The success of the Erfurt meeting largely resulted from Grünbaum's work in February 1970. By obtaining advance warning of the meeting, the Western powers were able to ensure its success by judiciously spreading rumours throughout East Germany. Normally, the DDR's Politburo had to use hired mobs to greet visiting foreign dignitaries. But on this occasion the East Germans came out spontaneously in their thousands to welcome Willy Brandt.

The whole affair was something of an internal embarrassment to the Politburo, and it finally convinced them of the public demand for diplomatic relations with the West. It was also Grünbaum's moment of glory, as Nagel expressed it. For perhaps the only time in his sordid career, the German had achieved something worthwhile.

"What you'd better do," Nagel said, "is get over to England and see this guy Wyman. Figure up a good excuse for being there and get clearance from the Firm. You'll find that Wyman's working in some third-rate sub-department somewhere in London. Find out what it is he does, and use it as an excuse to meet him. See what you can get out of him without letting on that we know about his trip to Rome, and we'll see about what to do next. Think you can do that?"

"Of course I can," Rawls snapped.

"Great. I'll send you all we've got on Wyman and the Krauts, and you can go as soon as you like."

"Okay," Rawls said, as he left the office.

Nagel knew that Rawls felt deeply insulted that a man of his proven ability should get a dreary assignment like this. That was precisely why Nagel had given it to him. A fat smirk crept across his face as Rawls left the room.

"Smart-assed prima donna," he chuckled.

CHAPTER NINETEEN

THE LONDON SKY WAS CLOUDLESS and crisp as Wyman strolled into Percy Street at 4.00 P.M. He entered the building, received another religious pamphlet from Mr Berkeley, and was greeted by Mrs Hobbes's vast backside as she bent over to switch on her vacuum cleaner at the top of the stairs. This gave Wyman an unfortunate view of her faded floral underwear and shattered stockings.

"Afternoon, Dr Wyman," Mrs Hobbes called out from between her legs. "How was your holiday?"

"Most refreshing, thank you, Mrs Hobbes," Wyman said, bravely ignoring her monstrous rump.

He climbed the stairs hurriedly and made straight for Owen's office.

"Good afternoon," Owen said, though his expression belied his words.

"Good afternoon."

"Well, how did it go? Did you make any progress?"

Wyman nodded.

"Things are going quite well."

He sat down and drew out a file from his briefcase. He opened the file and referred to it as he spoke.

"As far as anyone knows, the Germans are sticking to the notion that all the arrests were routine criminal affairs. There is no suggestion from the DDR that anyone is being detained on espionage charges. This would imply their determination that no one should know how the network was blown. Reichenbach was tried recently and jailed for two years for currency offences. No other trials have been announced yet, but we may expect similar news in due course.

"The difficulty in investigating this case is obvious. The only way we can find out what happened in Erfurt is by digging around in official circles. Of course, the only way this could ever be achieved was by using the Dovetail network."

"Yes," Owen said impatiently.

"The task has therefore been to find another source for the same information. Luckily, I have found one."

"Good show! Who is he?"

"I have code-named him Plato, and for the time being his identity must remain hidden."

"Even from me?" Owen asked indignantly.

"I'm afraid so. Plato insists upon anonymity. He is operating at a very high level in the SED, and his motives are purely mercenary. He believes that he can furnish the information we need, but at a very high price."

Owen's eyes narrowed in suspicion.

"How much?"

"Two million pounds sterling."

"That's ridiculous," Owen snapped. "I presume you made that quite clear."

"I did nothing of the sort," Wyman said calmly. "Plato is risking a great deal by acting for us, and he regards the figure as wholly justified."

"What exactly did you tell this Plato?"

"He knows that Dovetail's network has been blown, and that we want to know how it was blown. He does not know that it was an F-network, and he knows nothing about our suspicions."

"Can't he be persuaded to work for a more realistic figure?"

"He would regard it as a less realistic figure."

Owen frowned unhappily.

"Does Plato have any intention of defecting, now or later?"

"No," Wyman said. "As I explained, Plato is simply a mercenary. He is attracted to Western wealth, but not to the West itself. He is frequently involved in diplomatic work in Europe, so all we need to do is place the money in a special Swiss bank account which I have just opened."

"Out of the question," Owen said. "The Minister would never countenance it. Have you no idea of the pressure upon the Firm to reduce expenditure?"

"I have an extremely good idea," Wyman said coldly. "After all, I am a victim of it."

"Yes," Owen said in embarrassment. "I'm sorry."

"These are extraordinary circumstances, and they justify extraordinary expenditure."

"I doubt if the Minister would agree. Did you find out anything else in Europe?"

"Not much," Wyman said. "I tried to establish contact with Menger and Hahn. They're the only members of Dovetail's network who haven't yet been arrested."

"What happened?"

"No luck. Menger runs a shop somewhere, and Hahn works in a chemical plant. Short of entering the DDR, there is no way of establishing safe contact with them. Since they were only ever expected to deal with Dovetail, they know nothing about us."

"Perhaps if we sent someone in..." Owen speculated.

Wyman shook his head.

"Far too dangerous. Suicidal, in fact. It's almost certain that the SSD know about them. My theory is that they are being held out as bait for precisely this contingency."

"Put out a useless operative, pull in a British agent. I suppose you're right." Owen disliked having to make concessions to Wyman. "So what are we going to do?"

"Give Plato his money and see what happens. There is no alternative."

"No," Owen said emphatically. "We can't do that. There must be another way."

Wyman threw up his hands in frustration.

"Then what do you propose?" he demanded. "It occurs to me that parsimony will be the death of this organization."

"What about this end?" Owen asked. "If there really is someone here selling off information, can't we investigate at this end?"

"We can," Wyman said, "but it would be a mammoth task."

"I don't see why. All we need to do is check on who has access to the F-network file at this end. That will at least give us a list of suspects."

Wyman drummed his fingers on Owen's desk.

"The idea had occurred to me," he said patiently. "So I drew up such a list. There are thirty-five names on it. Each of these people has a secretary, and two or three juniors. Given the proximity of photocopiers to each office, anyone calling in on these people could have borrowed the file for long enough to duplicate the entries. Our short-list of suspects could therefore number some twelve hundred people. Where would you like to begin?"

Owen sank gloomily back into his chair.

"This is appalling," he said. "It makes a mockery of our security."

"It highlights the trust placed in the Firm's employees," Wyman said. "It needs just one mercenary, one agnostic, and the whole thing falls apart."

"Yes," Owen said weakly.

"I suggest you present the Minister with an extremely convincing case for giving Plato his two million pounds."

"He'll refuse," Owen said. "He's bound to."

"Why?"

"Because we're in an economic recession, that's why."

CHAPTER TWENTY

TEN DAYS AFTER MRS HOBBES had given him the information about Grünbaum, Bulgakov flew to East Germany by LOT, the Polish airline. At 11.45 A.M., his plane touched down at Erfurt airport.

Thuringia lies in the southwestern corner of the DDR, and Erfurt is its main city. It is a region of hazy blue mountains, dense green forests and graceful old towns.

Unlike many German cities, Erfurt has not been scarred by the twentieth century. For over seven hundred years its industrial community has thrived, and this prosperity is reflected in Erfurt's architectural splendour. There are streets and bridges dating back to the time of Martin Luther, who studied and became a monk here. The thirteenth-century Augustine monastery where Luther was ordained still stands, as does the cathedral where he gave his inaugural theological lecture.

Erfurt's stature as a centre of humanist thought went hand in hand with its economic strength. At one time Erfurt contained Germany's largest woad market, and one can still see the stately homes of those who grew rich from trading in that blue dye.

Nowadays, the dye trade has given way to the large industrial manufacturers, such as *VEB Kombinat Uniformtechnik* and *Kombinat Mikroelektronik*. Fortunately, Erfurt's history has not been defaced by the new industries, and it remains one of central Europe's most elegant cities.

As he got off his plane, Bulgakov was approached by a nervous young man with pimples and an abortive moustache.

"Major Bulgakov? I am Hauptmann Fichte. I have been assigned to be your assistant."

"Pleased to meet you, Hauptmann."

Bulgakov studied the young captain with amused contempt.

"We have a car waiting, Herr Major. The driver is collecting your luggage now."

Bulgakov was escorted to a black Wartburg near the airport terminal. They found the driver holding Bulgakov's suitcase.

"Shall I put it in the boot, Herr Major?" asked the driver. "Put it in the back seat," Bulgakov said. "I don't want to lose sight of it."

"Of course," said the captain. "I assume it contains vital documents."

"No," said Bulgakov. "It contains a set of monogrammed silk pyjamas I bought in Savile Row. It would cost a fortune to replace them."

The captain studied Bulgakov's face to see if he was joking, but he couldn't be sure. They got into the car and drove swiftly into the centre of Erfurt. On the way he tried clumsily to make conversation with Bulgakov.

"May I compliment you on your German, Herr Major. My superiors were wondering if you would need an interpreter."

Bulgakov ignored the captain's remark and continued to stare out of the window.

"How long have you been with the SSD, Hauptmann?"

"Eight months, Herr Major. May I ask...?"

"I was wondering how much contact you've had with my organization."

"Not much, Herr Major," Fichte said. He was puzzled and a little disconcerted by Bulgakov's manner.

"Clearly," Bulgakov smiled.

The captain flushed scarlet and abandoned his efforts to make conversation.

Within minutes the car arrived at a small, sober, eighteenth-century building just off the Futterstrasse. This was the Erfurt base of the SSD, East Germany's security service. Since November 1957, the *Staatssicherheitsdienst* has been run by Erich Mielke, the Minister for State Security. It was an indication of both Mielke's stature and that of his organization that he was given full membership of the DDR's Politburo in May 1976.

Western observers tend to underestimate the power and efficiency of the SSD, and it is widely regarded as little more than a handmaiden of the KGB. There is some justification for this view: the KGB have little regard for the Germans, and they refer contemptuously to the DDR as "the sixteenth republic of the USSR".

Within East Germany, however, the SSD wields enormous power, and it has scored some notable successes abroad.

Intelligence networks outside the DDR are organized by an SSD department known as the *Hauptverwaltung Aufklärung*, or HVA. It is run by Generalleutnant Markus Wolf, and was responsible for some of the most notorious spy scandals of the 1970s. Günther Guillaume, who became a personal aide of the West German Chancellor, Willy Brandt, was an employee of the HVA. So were Lothar-Erwin Lutze and his wife, whom Edgar Rawls had helped to expose. It was not until January 1979, when one of Wolf's officers defected to the West, that the full extent of HVA infiltration throughout West Germany became known.

But as far as Bulgakov was concerned, the SSD was a shower of amateurs, and he made little effort to conceal his feelings about Captain Fichte and his organization.

An office had been prepared for Bulgakov, and Fichte showed him to it. The major gave it a cursory glance and nodded.

"I trust this is all to the Major's satisfaction," Fichte said.

"There are two desks," Bulgakov observed. "Whose is the other one?"

"Mine, Herr Major. I assumed you would want me to be at hand."

"You assumed wrongly, Hauptmann. Is this where you normally work?"

"No, Herr Major. I have an office downstairs."

"Then you will stay there, I think." Bulgakov smiled and lit a cigarette. "You may remove that desk and replace it with a bed. I shall be staying here."

"But—but we had a room ready for you in the hotel, Herr Major. It really would be more comfortable—"

"You Germans have a taste for comfort, don't you?" Bulgakov grinned.

He noted with amusement that a small bead of perspiration was trickling down Fichte's face.

"I—I only meant—"

"I'm quite aware of what you meant, and I appreciate your concern. I will be quite happy here, thank you."

"Very good, Herr Major. I shall work downstairs. If you wish, you may contact me using the internal phone."

Bulgakov nodded and sat down behind his desk. He flicked the ash from his cigarette into a wastepaper basket. The captain noticed this and gave a little cough.

"I will have some ashtrays sent up immediately—"

"Do you know why I am here?" Bulgakov interrupted.

"All I know is that you wish to investigate the Grünbaum case, Herr Major."

"Is that all they've told you?"

The captain nodded.

"What do you know about Grünbaum? And for God's sake, sit down."

The captain took a seat.

"Very little, I'm afraid. I know he was a criminal, and it now appears that he was a spy as well."

"Spy!" Bulgakov spat the word out in disgust. "He was a *shavki*, Hauptmann. Just a petty informer. A nobody."

The captain frowned in confusion.

"In that case, I don't understand—"

"Why I'm here? The reason is this: the British have heard about Grünbaum's fate, and they are taking an unusual interest in it. Presumably they have drawn inferences from what happened. I want to know what those inferences are, and why they have drawn them. Do you understand?"

"Not entirely, I confess. What sort of inferences do you mean?"

Bulgakov smiled.

"I can't be more explicit, Hauptmann. There are some things even neighbours should not know."

"I understand, Herr Major."

"Splendid. You will now make a list of the things I require. Firstly, I want every scrap of available information concerning Grünbaum. I don't just want the SSD dossier: I think you will find that the *Volkspolizei* have a nice fat file on him, and I want to see it. I want to know exactly what happened on the night he died. Hence, I will also want to interview the police officer who went to arrest him. I believe his name is Mach."

"Very good, Herr Major."

Bulgakov drew an envelope from his pocket and gave it to Fichte.

"This contains a few other names. They are all

detainees of one sort or another, and I would like to see their files."

He leaned over and put out his cigarette in the wastepaper basket. The stub burned a small hole in the wickerwork.

"Will that be all, Herr Major?"

"Yes, Hauptman. Bring me all that information as soon as you receive it. Oh, and Hauptmann..."

"Yes, Herr Major?"

"I know that customs vary from country to country, but where I come from it is deemed advisable to have one's flies done up in the presence of a superior officer."

The captain stared down in horror.

"Oh! I do beg the Major's pardon, I—"

"Not at all, Hauptmann. Thank you."

The door closed and Bulgakov burst into laughter.

CHAPTER TWENTY-ONE

RAWLS' AEROPLANE LANDED at Heathrow Airport at lunchtime on May 21. Unlike Bulgakov, Rawls had no car waiting for him. Having extricated his suitcase from Heathrow's peculiar baggage retrieval system, he caught a Piccadilly Line underground train which took him into central London.

At Green Park Station, Rawls alighted and hailed a taxi for Grosvenor Square. At the US Embassy, he introduced himself to the attaché responsible for intelligence liaison. He was told that a hotel room had been reserved for him in Beaufort Street, and that arrangements had been made for him to visit MI6 headquarters that afternoon. The attaché was unaware of the precise nature of Rawls' visit, but he did know that the true reason was being kept secret from the British.

Rawls left his suitcase with the attaché, and he was

given a car to take him to MI6 headquarters. He was driven down Park Lane and Grosvenor Place, then through Victoria Street and into Parliament Square. After negotiating some heavy traffic, the driver took him over Westminster Bridge and stopped at County Hall, the headquarters of the Greater London Council.

Britain's intelligence-gathering organization has a variety of names. Publicly, it is known as MI6, or the SIS. Privately, it is known as the "Firm", or simply "Six". Its headquarters lie in the middle of a large roundabout connecting Lambeth Palace Road, York Road and Westminster Bridge Road. The building looks like a sawn-off step pyramid, and is known as the Ziggurat. It has been carefully elevated so that access from the roundabout is impossible. The only way in for visitors is by an enclosed walkway several floors up, linking the Ziggurat with the south block of County Hall.

Rawls entered County Hall and waved some impressive documents at the receptionist. He was taken upstairs and over into the Ziggurat, where he was introduced to an arid official.

"How do you do," the man drawled. "My name's Parfitt."

"Pleased to meet you," Rawls said.

"I understand that you'd like to visit GCHQ."

"Among other things. I'm with Anglo-US Liaison, as you know. At the moment, I'm involved with the preparations for the arms limitation talks. I've been sent over here to take soundings on how the British want us to handle the talks, and to find out what's been happening in the way of Warsaw Pact troop movements in Europe."

Rawls was referring to the next round of arms talks between the Americans and the Russians, to be held in Geneva the following July. The Russians were claiming that current US policy was aggressive and uncooperative, and that major concessions would be required if any sort of progress was to be made.

The Americans were replying that the Russians were indulging in more than their fair share of aggression, and they backed their case with lengthy accounts of Warsaw Pact exercises, as well as the setting-up of a new batch of rocket installations in Eastern Europe. GCHQ in Cheltenham was monitoring many of these new developments, and Rawls ostensibly wished to see their findings at first hand.

"I see," Parfitt said. "Well, that should provide no difficulties. We'll give you a permit to visit Cheltenham as from tomorrow. Is there anything else you would like?"

"Yeah, there's one more thing. We're particularly interested in what's happening in the DDR right now, especially in the southwest. I understand you've got a department here in London that specializes in DDR affairs, run by a guy called Owen."

"That's right. In fact, the area you're talking about is the speciality of a chap called Wyman, who works for Owen. If you like, I'll ask Wyman to prepare a report on the area for you, and we'll have it ready for you by the time you've returned from Cheltenham."

"No need, no need," Rawls said affably. "If it's okay, I'll speak to Wyman myself. It shouldn't take long."

"I don't see why not," Parfitt said. "They don't often get house-calls, so it should make a pleasant change for them. I'll fix up an appointment with Owen."

"Great," Rawls said.

They chatted amicably for another twenty minutes, and Parfitt prepared Rawls' permit to visit Cheltenham. The American then left the Ziggurat and drove back to Grosvenor Square.

CHAPTER TWENTY-TWO

"LUDICROUS," SAID THE MINISTER, "quite ludicrous."

He sniffed the bouquet of his Armagnac appreciatively, and drew a long puff from his Havana cigar.

"I know," Owen said. "But Wyman insists it's the only way."

"The man's living in a fantasy world. He's got to get a grip. Two million pounds—why doesn't he ask for Threadneedle Street while he's about it?"

"I've told him," Owen said. "But he's adamant that this chappie won't settle for less."

"He'll bloody well have to. How the hell could I justify that sort of expense to the PM?"

"I don't know. I explained to Wyman that the money simply isn't there, but he says there's no alternative."

"Nonsense," snorted the Minister. "What about internal inquiries? There must be a way of winkling out the information at home. More brandy?"

"Yes please," Owen said. "No, Wyman's right about that. The information we need is in East Germany, and we won't get it anywhere else."

"Can't we send someone out?"

"Too risky. If we do have a ferret in the Department, our man would walk straight into the hands of the SSD. They'd be waiting for him."

"And what if there isn't a ferret? We'd have paid out two million pounds for nothing."

"I agree, it would be a gamble."

"Gamble? It would be sheer folly."

The Minister blew out a long stream of yellow smoke and gazed contentedly at his glass of brandy.

"So what are we going to do?" Owen asked.

"Do? Shelve the investigation, I suppose."

"That could be very dangerous."

"We have no choice," said the Minister emphatically. "I can't justify forking out two million quid on this. As far as I'm concerned, if there's no other way of doing this, here endeth the lesson."

Owen nodded.

"Let us hope, then, that there really is no ferret."

The Minister settled back in his armchair.

"I'm sure there isn't, old chap," he said. "There's probably a simple explanation for those arrests, and we'll all be kicking ourselves when we find out."

"You're probably right," Owen said.

"Can't afford two million," said the Minister. "No way. There's a recession on, you know."

CHAPTER TWENTY-THREE

BULGAKOV SAT BEHIND HIS LARGE oak desk in Erfurt, reading some files. The SSD was being most helpful, and he now had virtually all the information he needed. Despite this, Bulgakov still regarded Captain Fichte with undisguised disdain. He found Fichte's enthusiasm as unpalatable as Fichte's acne. It was only when one was old enough to cultivate a healthy cynicism that one became proficient in this line of work, he reflected.

There was a hesitant tap on the door. "Come in," Bulgakov said. Fichte walked in and smiled timidly.

"Prisoner Reichenbach, Herr Major."

Bulgakov nodded solemnly.

"Bring him in, please."

A thin little man was pushed into the office at gunpoint.

"Thank you, Hauptmann. You may go."

Fichte shut the door behind him.

"Do sit down, Herr Reichenbach," Bulgakov said, with reptilian courtesy.

Reichenbach sat down nervously. He did not like Russians.

"What do you do for a living, Herr Reichenbach?"

"I'm a printer," Reichenbach said. "I've explained all this to the police..."

"Then you can explain it all again to me," Bulgakov smiled. "I am not a policeman."

He looked casually at Reichenbach's file and lit a Dunhill. "You were arrested on the eighteenth of December for illegal trading in foreign currency. Is that correct?"

Reichenbach nodded.

"And you were sentenced to five years' imprisonment."

"Yes, Herr Major."

"Did you make much profit out of these...activities?"

Reichenbach shrugged.

"A little. It's not as lucrative as you might suppose."

"Isn't it? How interesting."

Bulgakov blew smoke towards Reichenbach's face.

"I suppose you made a lot of contacts in this line of business."

"What do you mean?"

"Well, I'm sure there is quite a fraternity of criminals in Erfurt. You must have known a number of them."

"You're mistaken, Herr Major," Reichenbach said.

"I only did this occasionally, for my friends. I wasn't involved in anything, if that's what you mean."

"No?" Bulgakov's eyes twinkled with amusement. "You must be aware that there are black-marketeers here in Erfurt."

Reichenbach said nothing.

"These people," Bulgakov continued, "would be very interested in obtaining foreign currency, wouldn't they?"

"I suppose they would. But I had nothing to do with them."

"You only did it for your friends."

"That's right."

"How very noble of you." Bulgakov flicked ash onto the carpet. "So if I mentioned the name Grünbaum to you—Josef Grünbaum—I suppose that would mean nothing to you."

"No." Reichenbach shook his head.

"You have never heard of him?"

"No."

"Oh dear," Bulgakov sighed. "How disappointing. I had hoped that you were going to tell me all about him."

He ground out his cigarette.

"Some people," he continued, "think that you are connected with Grünbaum. They think you have known him for a long time. Why should they think that?"

"I don't know, Herr Major."

"These people think that you and Grünbaum were involved in more than just currency offences."

"Do they?"

"Yes, they do. Why should they suppose that, do you think?"

"I've no idea."

Bulgakov stood up and walked over to the window with his hands in his pockets. He looked out at a rainy spring morning.

"Does the name Gödel mean anything to you? It wouldn't, I suppose."

"No," said Reichenbach.

"Neumann? Kurt Neumann?"

"I'm afraid not, Herr Major. Who are these people?"

"Just...people."

Bulgakov returned to his desk and sat on it, directly in front of Reichenbach. He stared the prisoner straight in the face, as if he were trying to find something there.

"Funny, isn't it," Bulgakov said. "All these people think you know Grünbaum, and here you are, denying all knowledge of him."

He smacked his fist into Reichenbach's face. The prisoner toppled backwards.

"Get up."

Reichenbach got to his feet, shaking. Red syrup oozed down from his nostrils and onto his lips. He righted his chair and sat down.

"Let me ask you once more. What was your connection with Josef Grünbaum?"

"I've never heard of him," Reichenbach protested.

"I think you have," Bulgakov said. "Listen. Grünbaum is dead. He was shot while you were in prison. You will not betray him by telling me about him. Not now."

The German shook his head.

"I had never heard of Josef Grünbaum before you mentioned him to me. Truly."

Bulgakov hit him again. There was a muffled snap as Reichenbach's nose broke. Understandably, Reichenbach howled and clutched his face. He sobbed gently as Bulgakov lit another cigarette.

"When did they recruit you? Was it before 1958?"

"Nobody recruited me," Reichenbach blubbed. "I don't know what you're talking about. I'm just a printer—"

Bulgakov grabbed him by the throat and forced Reichenbach to stare into his eyes.

"If I wanted to," he said evenly, "I could kill you. Now. All you have to do is tell me about Grünbaum. I've told you, he's dead. You can't hurt him."

Reichenbach trembled like a beaten child.

"I swear I don't know what you're talking about. If I knew I'd tell you. Really. I don't—"

Bulgakov threw him against a wall and drove his fist into Reichenbach's groin. As the German sank to the floor, Bulgakov obligingly kneed him in the face.

"That's the price of loyalty," Bulgakov explained. "That's what they paid you for, isn't it?"

Reichenbach spat out little red fragments of teeth and ran a sleeve across his mouth.

"You're mistaken," he mumbled. "There's been a terrible mistake."

"Has there?" Bulgakov asked softly. "Listen, Reichenbach. I can beat you until your head falls apart. I can grind you to powder. I can do exactly what I please with you. Spies aren't protected by any laws, you know."

"Spies?" Reichenbach looked up in astonishment. "Are you saying I'm a spy?"

Bulgakov went behind his desk and sat down.

"You've been trained very well," he said. "I can see that. But it makes no difference in the end."

He looked at Reichenbach's broken face and red eyes. It always ends like this, he thought. They always die with that confused, incredulous look in their eyes. Presumably, no one ever dares to contemplate such a fate. Otherwise they would not do their work in the first place. They always think that it can't happen to them, and even when it does, they still refuse to believe it.

"It's going to be a long day," Bulgakov sighed. He said it in German, but he was really talking to himself.

CHAPTER TWENTY-FOUR

"**P**LATO WILL HAVE TO BE DROPPED," Owen said.

"Indeed," Wyman said. "May I ask why?"

"The Minister gave a number of reasons, and I agreed with him."

"I'm sure you did," Wyman said.

"First and foremost, there is the question of expense. Two million pounds is an outrageous sum. Had this Plato been prepared to settle for a more sensible figure, we might have taken a different view. If you are certain that Plato will not negotiate, then there is little we can do."

"Other than give him the money."

"Other than ignore him altogether," Owen snapped. "This leads on to the second point. How can we be certain of Plato's *bona fides*? You have given us no indication that Plato will fulfill his side of the bargain, apart from your belief in his honesty."

"After thirty years in this occupation, I think my opinions about the integrity of a source are worth slightly more than you suggest."

Owen shifted uncomfortably.

"I am not denigrating your abilities," he said. "I simply maintain that you haven't proved that Plato is worth the absurdly high fee he's demanding. Two million pounds for one informant is an unprecedented figure."

"As I recall," Wyman said, "there was a time when we would gladly have paid that figure and more, had it meant Philby's exposure, or that of Burgess. Why is it that we are always wise after the event in these matters?"

"But in this case, what is the event? That's my third point: we are still not satisfied that there is an infiltrator here in the Department."

"'Satisfied' is a rather odd term to use, isn't it?" Wyman said. "Until you can provide a better explanation for how the Dovetail network has been systematically dismantled, you must accept that we have a KGB plant in the Department. Surely, elementary logic would dictate this view."

"I am not talking about logic," Owen said. "I'm discussing practicalities. The exposure of the Dovetail network can probably be explained by other means. Henceforth, I would like you to explore *all* the possibilities, not just that of having an infiltrator in the Department."

Wyman sighed in frustration.

"As I explained to you, an investigation at this end would be an enormous task. It could take months, and I don't have months. You will recall that I am supposed to leave the Department at the end of June."

"If you haven't sorted it out by then," Owen said, "I shall find a replacement for you. If necessary, I'll do the work myself."

The idea of Owen having to plough through twelve hundred dossiers gave Wyman much private amusement.

"I'm sure you'd find the work most agreeable," he said.

"Of course I wouldn't," Owen barked. "But at least it wouldn't mean giving absurd sums of money to some greedy German, with no guarantee of getting anything in return. In the meantime, you will start the investigation, and we'll see how you progress."

"Very well," Wyman said. "There appears to be no alternative. I only hope that the Minister won't have cause to regret his decision."

"If you do your job properly," Owen said acidly, "he'll have no cause to regret it. Will he?"

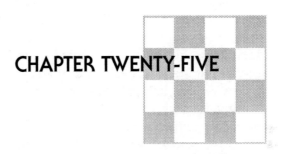

CHAPTER TWENTY-FIVE

"**M**R RAWLS? HOW DO YOU DO. I'm Michael Wyman."

They shook hands, and Rawls was escorted into Wyman's office. He had just spent the last ten minutes convincing Mr Berkeley that he was not an American tourist, and he'd then been sent upstairs with a pamphlet entitled "Prepare To Meet Thy Maker".

Rawls waved the pamphlet at Wyman.

"Does everyone get one of these?"

"Oh yes," Wyman smiled. "Mr Berkeley's a very generous man. I say, I haven't seen that one before. May I take a look?"

"Sure," Rawls said. He began to wonder what he had let himself in for.

"My word," Wyman exclaimed, "this is good stuff. Mr Berkeley obviously doesn't worship the God of

Mercy. Apparently, we're all sunk in the Pit of Depravity, and the Lord will smite us with everlasting boils and sores."

"Is that a fact?" said Rawls.

He sat down and glanced swiftly at his surroundings. They confirmed his worst prejudices. Hundreds of documents, all of them classified material, were strewn casually about the desk and floor like Weimar banknotes. Several half-full cups of tea had penicillin mould floating in them, the ashtrays were overflowing, and according to the calendar on the wall it was still January.

Some books were heaped carelessly on a shelf above a rusty filing cabinet. Rawls read the titles: *Das Kontinuum* by Hermann Weil, *The Journal of Symbolic Logic 1962*, a book of Giles cartoons and *The Theory of Numbers* by R. Dedekind.

"I understand you're into logic," Rawls said.

"I dabble," Wyman said. "Quite interesting, once you've got into it."

"Yeah, I'm sure. Well, I suppose you're wondering why I've come to see you."

"I was rather surprised," Wyman confessed.

"It's about these arms talks scheduled for July. You've heard about all that, I guess..."

"Very little, in fact."

"Well, we'd like everyone to turn up in Geneva, but nobody's too sure about it at the moment. You see, Mr Wyman—sorry, I should have said 'Doctor', shouldn't I?"

"'Michael' will do fine."

"Okay, Michael. The Russians claim we're jeopardizing the talks by manufacturing too many tactical missiles. They're right, but that isn't going to stop us making them."

"So what are you going to do?"

"We're going to prove that the Russians are being as aggressive as anybody else, and that we're just taking defensive measures. So far, the case looks pretty good: we know they've been conducting a whole series of large-scale military manoeuvres throughout the Iron Curtain countries. We've also got reports of new rocket installations in East Germany."

"And where do I fit in?"

"I understand you specialize in the southwest corner of the DDR."

"That's right."

"Well, I was wondering if you've heard anything that might be of help to us: troop movements, military convoys, that kind of thing."

"I see. Offhand, I couldn't tell you. We do get reports on all that business, and we keep them upstairs. If you like, I could look through them to see if there's anything of interest to you."

"I'd be very grateful if you could."

"How soon do you need them? I could get a file completed in twenty-four hours, or if you're in a rush, I could do it now."

"I'd appreciate getting them today, if that won't be too much trouble."

"No, not at all," Wyman said genially. "If you don't mind waiting here, I could run off photocopies in about fifteen minutes."

"That'd be great."

"Splendid," Wyman beamed.

He stood up and opened the door. Mrs Hobbes was outside, emptying the dust-bag of her Hoover. Wyman turned to Rawls. "Care for a cup of tea, old man?"

"Prefer a coffee, if that's OK."

"I say Mrs Hobbes, any chance of a coffee for my guest?"

"Of course, Dr Wyman. How does he like it?"

"How do you like it?"

"Black, no sugar," Rawls said.

"Black, no sugar," Wyman said.

"Right you are, love," Mrs Hobbes said. "Oh, Dr Wyman? Can I do your office today? It really needs it. You haven't let me in for *weeks*."

"Some other time, Mrs Hobbes. Things are rather busy at the moment. See you in a jiffy, old chap," he said to Rawls.

Wyman went upstairs. Rawls waited for the leisurely footsteps to disappear before he got up and crossed the room.

"'Old chap'," he grunted. "'Old man'. Asshole."

There were four filing cabinets in Wyman's office. One was labelled A-K, another L-Z. Carpet fluff poked out from under them, indicating that they had been there for some time. The third was a small table-top cabinet labelled "M.o.D. Code Compendia 1974-79".

The fourth cabinet was more promising. It was simply labelled "Thuringia", and it was locked. Rawls went over to Wyman's desk and opened the top drawer. It contained pens, writing paper and an assortment of elastic bands and paper-clips. He opened the top side-drawer and found a paperback entitled *How to Play the*

Flute, by Arthur Schopenhauer, and a couple of spare ribbons for Wyman's battered old Olivetti typewriter.

The drawer below contained a box of matches, an invitation to a Fellows' Dinner, and a small bunch of keys. Rawls took the keys and returned to the filing cabinet marked "Thuringia".

The third key opened the cabinet. The top drawer contained entries from A to F. He opened the drawer below and looked up "Grünbaum". The file was lengthy, but Rawls saw what he needed in the opening lines of the first page:

"GRÜNBAUM, Josef 1930—(See also GÖDEL Otto; NEUMANN, Kurt; REICHENBACH, Gunther; HAHN, Friedrich; MENGER, Moritz) Leader of network ERF1O6F."

Rawls copied this into his pocket-diary and closed the filing cabinet. He returned to Wyman's desk and was just about to replace the keys when he heard a rattle behind him.

"Black, no sugar," said Mrs Hobbes. Her blood-red lipstick curled in a benevolent smile.

"That's right," Rawls said. "Thank you."

"Don't get many visitors here, especially Americans."

"So I hear."

She looked around the office and frowned.

"Disgusting, isn't it? I'm sure Dr Wyman's a very clever man, but he still needs to learn about hygiene. Just look at those cups."

"Yeah. Pretty bad, huh?"

"He never lets me in here, that's the trouble. Always says he's too busy. Only costs five minutes to have your office cleaned, that's what I tell him. He says it only takes four minutes to destroy the world. Funny man, our Dr Wyman."

"Yeah. A real scream."

"Well, I must be getting along. Nice talking to you, love."

She shuffled out of the room. Rawls gazed at her bloated backside in horrified disbelief. Only the British, he reflected, could employ somebody so repugnant in their intelligence offices.

"Christ," he muttered, "is this MI6 or London Zoo?" He put the keys back in Wyman's desk and was struck by a flash of inspiration. He took out one of Wyman's spare typewriter ribbons and exchanged it for one in Wyman's Olivetti. The used ribbon then went into Rawls' pocket.

He noticed Wyman's note-pad. There was nothing written on the top sheet, since Wyman tore pages out after writing them. But Rawls tore off the top two sheets anyway and consigned them to his pocket.

He was halfway through the worst cup of coffee he had ever tasted when Wyman returned, brandishing a wad of photocopies.

"Here you are, old boy," Wyman said. "There's nothing terribly exciting here, but some of the activities in Mühlhausen last February might interest you."

"Great. Thanks very much. I'd better be going now. I'm supposed to be meeting someone at the American Club at five."

"Taxi or tube?"

"Which is quicker?"

"At this time of day, the tube. Take the Central Line westbound at Tottenham Court Road and change at Oxford Circus onto the Victoria Line southbound. It's just down the road from Green Park tube station."

"Thanks. I'm much obliged."

"Not at all. Cheerio."

"Goodbye."

Rawls walked out and hailed the first taxi he saw.

CHAPTER TWENTY-SIX

THE NIGHT WAS COOL, damp and slimy, and so was the Thames. Rawls strolled westwards along Chelsea Embankment and watched the leisurely slurp of the river some twenty feet below him. On the other side of the water huddled a dark amorphous jungle called Battersea Park.

His luminous watch read 2.17 A.M. He quickened his pace as he passed Albert Bridge. About halfway down Cheyne Walk, he paused and turned around. There were footsteps about fifteen feet behind him. Someone was following him home.

He crossed the road onto the north side and broke into a run. The soft footsteps behind him also crossed the road. From the corner of his eye Rawls saw the silhouette of his pursuer. There were two courses open to Rawls: he could either make a straight run for home or he could tackle the other man. He took the latter option.

Rawls tore round the corner of Beaufort Street and saw two cars parked there. He crouched between the vehicles and waited for the muted footsteps to catch him up.

The other man turned the corner, saw no sign of Rawls, and slowed down apprehensively. Rawls waited for about two seconds while the pursuer passed the cars, and then he sprang at the man's back.

Rawls was good at unarmed combat. He held a black belt, second dan in ju-jitsu. He did not expect the other man to be more proficient than that. With practised skill, Rawls jabbed his left fist hard into the kidney of the unknown man. Understandably, the pursuer arched back in pain, and Rawls' right arm closed around his throat.

Unfortunately, the other man was also proficient in the martial arts. Despite his discomfort, he knew how to deal with such attacks. His right arm smashed a back elbow-jab deep into Rawls' solar plexus. Winded, Rawls crumpled forward and allowed his opponent's left arm to reach back and grab his hair. The pursuer flicked forward and pulled hard. Rawls flew over him and landed on his back, with both feet pointing towards the King's Road.

Just as Rawls hit the pavement, his opponent twisted round and pinned a knee across Rawls' throat.

"I think that's enough for one night, Mr Rawls," Bulgakov said calmly. "Don't you? I only wanted to talk."

"Yes," Rawls gurgled.

"Good," smiled the Major.

He stood up and helped Rawls off the pavement.

"Holy shit," Rawls croaked. "Next time, just say hello, will you?"

Rawls limped back to his hotel in Beaufort Street, accompanied by Bulgakov. The two men had first met in Chile in the early 1970s. Rawls had been working for the CIA's Clandestine Services Department as an operational link-man between his own organization and the International Telephone and Telegraph Company. Like the CIA, ITT was working to undermine the regime of Salvador Allende, but unlike the CIA, its motives were purely financial. ITT had assets worth $150 million in Chile which were threatened by Allende's policy of expropriation.

ITT pursued an independent programme of subversion in Chile, using its own resources and agents, until Wilson V. Broe stepped in. Broe was the chief of the Western Hemisphere Division of the CIA's Clandestine Services, and therefore Rawls' boss. Through Broe's intervention, ITT and the CIA worked in concert in Chile. Rawls was sent out to organize the collaboration.

While Rawls was helping to overthrow the Allende regime, Bulgakov was helping to prop it up. It was Bulgakov's first major assignment with the First Chief Directorate; his job was to help reorganize Allende's confused and inept counter-intelligence system, and to help disseminate propaganda and disinformation.

Both Bulgakov and Rawls recalled their cynical

encounters in the drab cafés on the back streets of Santiago late in 1972. Both men had known that Allende's regime would topple; Rawls had commiserated with Bulgakov for having been given a hopeless mission. The Russian had been asked to give first-aid to a dying man. The American was there to administer the last rites.

"You haven't changed much," Bulgakov said.

"Nor have you," said Rawls. "Where did you learn the ju-jitsu? I thought I was pretty good, but…"

"There's a training establishment on Metrostroevskaya Street," Bulgakov said. "I got my black belt there. You shouldn't have jumped at me."

"Too damned right I shouldn't," Rawls grunted. He nursed his throat ruefully. "Anyway, what did you want to see me about?"

Bulgakov smiled and pulled out a Dunhill.

"I thought you'd never ask. I want to know what you're doing here."

"You know why I'm here," Rawls said.

"No." Bulgakov shook his head. "I know why you claim to be here. You're supposed to be helping with the groundwork for the arms talks, and visiting people at GCHQ. I don't believe a word of it."

"It's true," Rawls said.

"GCHQ is in Cheltenham. What are you doing in London?"

"I'm here to see the Changing of the Guard at Buckingham Palace. Then I'm going to see Trafalgar

Square, the Tower of London and, if time permits, Madame Tussauds."

"Very droll, Rawls," Bulgakov said. "Listen, I think I know why you're here."

"Of course you do. I've just told you."

"It's about that fool Grünbaum, isn't it?"

"Who?"

"Don't be boring, Rawls. Please."

"I didn't think I was here to entertain you, Bulgakov."

Bulgakov peered at Rawls through a cloud of smoke.

"You think Grünbaum was exposed by a *nash* in MI6, don't you?"

"What do you think?"

"I think someone has made an enormous error."

"Yeah? Fascinating."

"As I understand it, you and the British think there were other arrests relevant to Grünbaum's death. Neumann, for example."

"What about him?"

"The Germans say he was put in the psychiatric hospital for legitimate medical reasons. You don't believe that."

"Eastern governments regularly put people they don't like in psychiatric hospitals. Your buddies in the KGB just love locking people up inside the Serbsky Institute. If they don't agree with us, they must be crazy, isn't that the idea?"

Bulgakov shrugged.

"Such things do happen," he conceded. "But not this time. Really, Neumann is a genuine lunatic. He was put away because he was a real danger to the community."

"I've heard that line before," Rawls grinned.

The Russian sighed.

"I'm not making much progress, am I? Believe me, Rawls, there is no *nash*. Truly. I don't understand why Grünbaum's death and the other arrests should lead you to suppose there is."

Rawls gave Bulgakov the sort of look that most people reserve for visitors from Mars.

"You expect me to believe that?"

"I do."

"Okay," Rawls said. "Two questions: One: how did you find out I was here and what I'm here for?"

"Very well. The London *rezidentura** noticed the departure of Michael Wyman for Europe on May 11. Wyman made inquiries about Grünbaum and the others in Rome, Paris and Vienna, and some of those inquiries were reported back here. We had known about Grünbaum for years, and we couldn't understand why the British were making such a fuss about his death. We noted your arrival on May 21, and you were seen visiting Wyman's office. Wyman's people have nothing to do with GCHQ, so we guessed what you were after. Does that satisfy you?"

"It'll do," Rawls said. "Okay. Question number two: if Grünbaum really was nobody in particular, and if I'm chasing my own ass, why the hell should that bother you?"

Bulgakov blew out a long puff of smoke and smiled serenely at Rawls.

"Because if you believe this rubbish, Rawls, you will

---

* *Rezidentura*: The KGB section within each Russian embassy.

probably go to East Germany to investigate. Am I right?"

Rawls said nothing.

"And if you go to East Germany there will be trouble."

"How come?"

The Russian looked upwards in exasperation.

"There is always trouble when you and your friends visit the DDR, or any other Socialist country. Right now, with the arms talks coming up, we can't afford any silly scandals. You people are experts at creating unnecessary difficulty. There is no need for any of it."

"Now you're being boring."

"There is no KGB *nash* in MI6, Rawls. There really isn't."

Rawls nodded reflectively.

"Just one more question, Major."

"What is it?"

"If there really was a Soviet ferret somewhere in the Firm—just supposing—would you say anything different from what you're saying now?"

Bulgakov smiled.

"No," he said. "I suppose I wouldn't."

"Right," said Rawls.

CHAPTER TWENTY-SEVEN

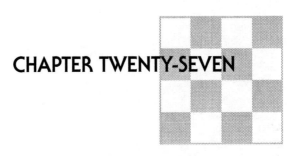

MEMO:22/5   From: Wyman
                             To: Owen

Re: FINGERPRINT TESTS ON GRUNBAUM FILE

New Scotland Yard laboratories confirm that the
new prints on the Grünbaum file and the keys to its
cabinet match those on Rawls' coffee-cup. This and
the switched typewriter ribbon form conclusive
proof of CIA interest in the Grünbaum affair. We
may assume that Rawls has been assigned to investigate the case.

CHAPTER TWENTY-EIGHT

THE MINISTER'S CLUB SERVED excellent meals. Over dinner, Owen tried to explain Wyman's latest memo. However, the subject became submerged beneath the hors d'oeuvre (caviare served in ice and eaten with the Club's finest crystal spoons, washed down with a bottle of chilled Montbazillac 1957). They moved on to their main course, Filet de Bouef à la Périgourdine (beef with truffles, braised in Madeira, glazed and served with slices of Foie Gras), which they lubricated with a bottle of Nuits-Saint-Georges 1959. They finished with a dessert of Pont L'Evêque cheese and a bottle of Saint-Emilion 1955.

After this they both belched discreetly and sat down in their armchairs with their glasses of brandy.

"Cognac, this time," said the Minister. "Champagne VSOP, mind you. Still, the Armagnac has something which—"

"About the Americans," Owen said.

"Ah, yes. Nosey devils. We can't have them poking around."

"That's precisely what they are doing."

"Yes. Are you sure this Rawls fellow was looking specifically for the Grünbaum file? I mean, it could have been accidental—"

"There's no question about it," Owen said. "His fingerprints were plastered all over the filing cabinet and Wyman's keys. The Grünbaum file was in a lower drawer, so if Rawls had been searching at random he would have looked in the top drawer as well. There were no fingerprints on any of the top files, which indicates that Rawls knew exactly what he was looking for. The CIA clearly know what's going on."

"How very bloody," said the Minister. "Very bloody indeed. You know, I really can't stand the Americans. They're so noisy and vulgar."

"How are we going to deal with them?"

"Mmmm. Good question. Got any ideas?"

Owen shook his head.

"The only thing we can do is to seek out the infiltrator before they do. Otherwise there'll be a scandal of epic proportions."

"Yes," said the Minister. "Highly unpleasant. The thing is, they've been on my back for some time about security in London. They claim we're not strict enough, the impudent peasants. I suppose we're going to have to find this blasted ferret."

"Yes," Owen said.

"And how are we going to do that?" Owen paused uncomfortably.

"I only know of one way," he said.

"Well?"

"We must give Plato his two million pounds."

The Minister coughed angrily.

"For God's sake, not *that* again."

"I'm afraid so."

The Minister ran a distressed hand across his forehead.

"The PM will flay me alive," he said.

"And what will happen if the Americans find the infiltrator?"

"Departmental genocide," the Minister said. "It would make a Stalinist purge look like natural wastage."

"So we have no choice."

"I suppose not. Damn those bloody Americans. Why do they always get involved?"

"I'm afraid they don't trust us. They think we're inept."

"And what right have they to think that?" the Minister shouted. "God knows, they've put their foot in it often enough."

Owen sighed.

"Heaven knows what Rawls has already found out."

"Who is he, this Rawls? Is he any good?"

"He's a typical CIA whiz kid," Owen said disdainfully. "Efficient. Good record. All in all, a bloody nuisance."

"What made Wyman suspicious of him?"

"We don't get many Yanks calling in at the Department. And who on earth would want to see Wyman?"

The Minister slurped his brandy and emitted another muffled belch.

"How did the Americans find out about all this, do you think?"

"We can only guess," Owen said. "They probably have their own sources. But it could just be that one of Wyman's European contacts talked a bit too loudly."

"Wyman! That man really is the limit. It's a pity we didn't get rid of him sooner."

"I'm inclined to agree with you," Owen said. "Still, without him, we'd never have heard about the ferret."

"Ferret, indeed," the Minister sneered. "It will probably turn out to be an office junior who talks too much in his pub."

"Perhaps. But he must be found, whoever he is."

"I suppose you're right," said the Minister. He groaned in dismay. "Two million pounds. It's obscene, Owen. Obscene. I'd have enough trouble justifying that sort of figure at the best of times, but right now… who the hell is this Plato? Doesn't he read the newspapers? Someone ought to tell him we're in an economic recession."

He gazed sadly into his glass of Cognac.

CHAPTER TWENTY-NINE

MOST PEOPLE ARE UNAWARE that the CIA is not the United States' largest intelligence agency. That title belongs to the National Security Agency.

The NSA is the biggest and most efficient intelligence system the Americans have yet devised. It was founded in 1952, and employs approximately 25,000 people and operates over 200 intelligence posts throughout the world. Despite its size, few people have ever heard of it. Its existence was virtually unknown outside the US until 1960, when two of its employees, Bernon Mitchell and William Martin, defected to the USSR.

The NSA avoids publicity by acting solely as an eavesdropping facility. It employs few "secret agents", and engages in no paramilitary activity, but its headquarters at Fort Gordon G. Meade, Maryland, house the most sophisticated eavesdropping equipment ever created. It can listen automatically to one million simultaneous telephone calls, and it can overhear and record telecommunications virtually anywhere in the world. As well as intercepting messages, it runs a team of highly skilled cryptologists. It was the home of one of these cryptologists that Rawls visited on the evening of May 25.

Harvey Everett James was a friendly little US major in his mid-thirties. He was married to a fragrant, thirteen-stone woman called Edna, who stood a full seven inches taller than he. This improbable union resulted in six noisy children, and their home life was a model of suburban bliss.

When Rawls arrived at the house, he was shown in by Edna and escorted to the lounge. He found James surrounded by four children. They were studying a toy racing car.

"The motor's broken, Sammy. It's got nothing to do with the battery."

"It's the battery, Dad. The same thing happened last week, and—"

"It's not the same thing. Something's broken in there, you can hear it rattling around. Hi, Ed."

"Hello, Harvey," Rawls said.

"You any good with toy cars?" James asked hopefully.

"Sorry," Rawls said, eyeing the children with distaste. "It's a long time since I used one."

"I'm afraid its broken, kids. I'll try and fix it later."

"It's the battery, Dad. Why don't you put a new one in?"

"Believe me, it's broken. A new battery won't do any good."

"Why don't you try?"

"I know a broken motor when I see one, Darren, that's why. Anyway, I've got to talk to Mr Rawls now."

"I bet it's the battery."

James took Rawls to another room.

"Kids are wonderful things," he sighed. "Some of the time."

"Maybe," Rawls said. "How did it go?"

"Okay," James said. He passed a small file of documents over to Rawls. "It's all written down, but I'll tell you anyway."

"Great," Rawls said.

"First, the notepaper. We had some trouble with that, because Wyman has lousy handwriting, and his pen didn't make much of an impression on the paper below. The only thing we could make sense of was a code: G2H-17-493. I'll explain that in a minute.

"Next, the typewriter ribbon. That was no problem: we got a nice print-out from it. This guy Wyman writes his memos out on it, and we've pieced together some of those. As you'll see, there's a lot of talk about someone code-named Plato. It seems that Plato's got a special Swiss bank account. That gave us the clue to the first code.

"The memos also say that Wyman was in Switzerland recently, so I took a long shot and guessed that G2H-17-493 was the bank account number. I was right."

"That's good guessing," Rawls said.

"Not really. I've dealt with Swiss banks before. The

number had a familiar sort of look, so I ran it through the computer and it tied in with the Banque Internationale Descartes in Geneva. The code breaks down like this: G2H is the bank's own identifying code. The 17 is the number of the manager in charge of this account: that's a Monsieur Emile Barthes. The 493 tells you that this is the 493rd file under Monsieur Barthes' control."

"I'm impressed," Rawls said. "I know it's an asshole question, but how come you guys know all about Swiss banks?"

"We know about a lot of things," James grinned. "You'd be surprised."

"I guess I would. Okay, so whose is the 493rd file?"

"Ah, there I can't help you. That's what Swiss banks are all about, Ed. All I know is that G2H-17-493 belongs to someone called Plato."

"Okay, so tell me all about Plato."

"The memos aren't too explicit about this, but I would guess that he's an East German working for the Brits. They use Greek philosophers' names for all the really juicy contacts they pick up in the SED. We know about a Zeno, an Aristotle and an Epicurus, but we've never heard of Plato. I guess he's new."

"Who are these guys?"

"They're big, but they're tricky. Usually they're members of the Party Central Committee or something like that, and they're often paying their way towards an easy defection. The problem is that they want to stay independent, and sometimes they get funny ideas about who's boss. They're expensive and they've got to be handled carefully. The Brits usually give them enough rope to hang themselves, and then blackmail them into doing what they want. It doesn't always work, and Plato sounds like an expensive guy."

"How much?"

"One of the memos says two million sterling. That's a lot of cash, especially for the Brits. My guess is he's got something very important to sell."

"I know he has," Rawls said. "What this amounts to is that the only people who know Plato's identity are Wyman and the manager of the bank."

"You've got it," James said.

"Wyman won't talk," Rawls said. "So how do I get the bank manager to sing?"

James grinned impishly.

"I thought you'd want to know that, so I got something ready for you in the file."

"What's it say?"

"There's a 1974 treaty between us and the Swiss that allows us to get a look at accounts of US felons if they can only be arrested on a tax rap."

"Like Al Capone?"

"Right. It's all in the file: if you can make out that you're from the Internal Revenue Service and claim that this account holds illegally obtained US dollars, they've got to let you take a look at it."

"But the account doesn't contain US dollars. Plato's getting paid in sterling, so it's none of our business."

"No problem," James said. "Claim that the money was laundered in France—the file explains how it's done. Also, I think there's a way of getting the bank to let you see the account without having to take it to the

Swiss Bankers' Federation. Take a look at the file and see what you think."

"You bet I will," Rawls said. "You've done a great job, Harvey. Thanks."

"Pleasure," James said.

A toy car whirred into the room, hotly pursued by James's children.

"See, Dad?" they bawled triumphantly. "It was the battery."

CHAPTER THIRTY

NAGEL HAD A RARE TALENT. He could produce more crumbs from one small sandwich than anyone else at Langley. The crumbs ran down Nagel's tie, tumbled onto his desk and scattered across the carpet like a small hailstorm. Rawls watched him in disgust.

"Okay," Nagel said through a mouthful of salami, "how was your trip?"

"A lot happened," Rawls said. "I think we've bought into something much bigger than we originally guessed."

"Oh yeah?" Nagel sounded unimpressed.

"Yeah. I think there's a ferret in the Firm."

Nagel nodded, frowned and stared disbelievingly at Rawls. "Shee-yit!" he exclaimed. He pushed a button on his intercom. "Miss Langer? Who got these fucking sandwiches?"

"I got them, sir," said a nasal female voice.

"You know I take mustard in my salami sandwiches, Miss Langer, don't you?"

There was a pause.

"Yes, sir, I do."

"Well," Nagel growled, "why isn't there any flicking mustard in my fucking sandwich? How do you account for this?"

"I'm sorry, Mr Nagel. I forgot."

"You forgot?" Nagel howled. "Forgot? Meat without mustard is naked, Miss Langer. Naked."

"Yes, Mr Nagel."

"Do you ever 'forget' to dress yourself in the morning?"

"No, Mr Nagel."

"There are laws against indecent exposure, Miss Langer."

"Yes, Mr Nagel."

Remember that."

"Yes, Mr Nagel."

He switched off.

"Where were we? Oh yeah. So you think there's a ferret in MI6. Well, start at the beginning."

Nagel slurped a large mouthful of coffee and emitted a deep, satisfied belch.

"I saw Wyman at his department," Rawls said. "He's a prick. Absent-minded, disorganized, messy, you name it. Anyway, I gave him a load of horseshit about needing to know about troop movements in the DDR. He believed all that, and while he was upstairs getting the info, I switched his typewriter ribbon, got a copy off his notepad and looked inside his filing cabinet.

"Grünbaum ran an F-network in Erfurt. The file gave the other members of the network, and I checked those out at home. Three of them got busted before Grünbaum did, and of course that just doesn't happen with F-networks.

"After I left Wyman's place I sent the notes and the typewriter ribbon back here using the diplomatic bag. I know a guy at the NSA who's into decoding typewriter printouts and all that kind of crap, and he did a nice job for me. But I didn't have to wait for that to find out what was happening. A KGB man called Bulgakov paid me a visit in London."

"That's cute," Nagel observed. "How does he figure in this?"

"I knew him in Chile. He's a smart cookie, but he ballsed-up this time. You see, he heard about my visit to Wyman, and he thought I knew the whole story. I didn't, of course, but I managed to string him along until he told me everything I needed to know."

"Which was...?"

"When London found out what had happened to Grünbaum's network, the warning lights started flashing. Wyman was Grünbaum's case officer, and it's his job to find out how the network got burned. But with an F-network there's only one explanation."

"A ferret? Right. That explains why Wyman was making all those unofficial inquiries in Europe."

"Exactly. Now, Bulgakov wants us to think that this is all baloney. He says he knows we suspect there's a ferret in the Firm, and he says we've got it all wrong. According to Bulgakov, all the arrests in East Germany were for genuine criminal offences. Can you believe that? I'm supposed to accept that several people in Germany are busted as genuine criminals, and it's just coincidence that they're all in the same spy network."

"Why did Bulgakov tell you all this?" Nagel asked.

"He says he wants to avoid trouble. He thinks we're going to send someone into Germany, and that'll cause a scandal, screwing up the arms talks."

Nagel nodded.

"It's possible," he said. "Stranger things have been known."

"Do you think he's kosher?" Nagel asked.

"I don't think he is," Rawls said. "After all, he's not really asking us to do him a favour, and he certainly isn't offering us anything. Anyway, the Brits are convinced there's a ferret in MI6, and they're the guys who usually get complacent about these things."

"What did the typewriter ribbon say?"

"It confirms and elaborates upon what Bulgakov told me. Apparently, the Brits have got their own ferret high up in the SED somewhere. He's some kind of mercenary, and they've code-named him Plato. Whoever he is, he's big. They've given him a bank account in Geneva, and the word is that he'll pick up two million sterling if he finds out how Grünbaum's people got blown."

"Two million?" Nagel said. "I'm impressed."

"So was I. Anyway, that's pretty well all I know. Where do I go from here?"

Nagel leaned back in his chair, lit a cigarette and paused for thought.

"The trouble with the Brits is that all their dirt becomes public," he mused. "Every time they find a ferret, the Press gets hold of the story, questions get asked in the House of Commons, all shit breaks loose. They just don't know how to deal with the sons of bitches."

"And how do you deal with them?"

"You burn 'em, boy. Burn 'em."

"And that isn't public?"

"Not if you do it the right way. No need to blow their balls off, if you see what I mean. There are other ways."

"So I hear," Rawls said drily.

Nagel grinned.

"You can do better than that," he said.

"Do I have any choice?"

"No. We've got to find the London ferret and deal with him before the Brits get there first."

"We?"

"Okay. You."

"Thought so."

"Now don't get coy with me, boy. You know what's required. Do you think Wyman stands any chance of getting him first?"

"No," Rawls said. "Wyman is a jerk. He's out of date."

"Don't underestimate Wyman. Some of these Brits are smart operators."

"Not Wyman," Rawls said emphatically. "The only reason I got all this information is because Wyman's security is so lousy. He's a prick, and I'm not the only one who says that, I checked up on Wyman: his people are firing him fairly soon. You don't fire good operators."

"I guess not," Nagel said. "But what about this mystery man Plato? What if he gives Wyman the word?"

"That's the real problem," Rawls agreed. "We need to keep an eye on that Swiss bank account. If anything goes in, then we'll be sure that Plato's onto something."

Once more, Nagel paused for thought.

"Can we be sure that it'll definitely be Wyman who pays the two million into the account?"

"Pretty certain," Rawls said. "It's big business, opening up one of those accounts. If Plato's stuck in East Germany, someone must be acting as his agent. That must be Wyman, because we know that Wyman's already had dealings with the bank. Given that, and the fact that Wyman wants the whole thing kept as quiet as possible, we can assume that he'll be paying in the two million."

"Right," Nagel said. "I don't know how feasible this is, but we might be able to keep an eye on the bank. Put a camera outside, or something."

"So?"

"So if Wyman walks into the bank, he'll be photographed and we'll know about it."

"Okay. We've got pictures of Wyman already. Getting a camera hook-up shouldn't be any problem. So what do I do?"

Nagel grinned slyly.

"You, my boy, are going back to Europe. Go to East Germany and find out what happened to Grünbaum. Try and find out who this fucking ferret is."

"I might need to know who Plato is, and right now there's only one way of doing that."

"How?"

"Go to the bank in Geneva and get the name from the manager of the account. I know a way of doing that, but I'll need help."

"What sort of help?"

"Some phony passports and ID."

"ID?"

"I'll need to make out that I'm working for the IRS. The story will be that Plato's bank account contains illegal US dollars."

"Will they believe that?"

"I think so. Do I get the ID?"

Nagel nodded.

"Yeah, why not. As and when Wyman shows up in Geneva, I'll put the word out to all the US embassies in Europe. As long as you stay tuned wherever you are, you'll know exactly what's happening. Okay?"

"Fine," Rawls said.

"Wonderful. I can see you're going to have a great time on this one."

Rawls gazed at him blankly.

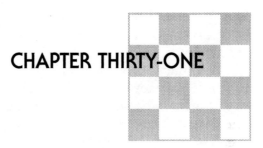

CHAPTER THIRTY-ONE

"**C**OME IN," OWEN SAID.

Wyman sat down in front of Owen's desk.

"I passed your memo on to the Minister," Owen said.

"Indeed."

"Yes." Owen coughed. "In the light of these new developments, the Minister and I both feel that the Grünbaum case should be reopened."

Wyman stifled a yawn.

"And...?"

"Well...damn it, we can't have the bloody Americans poking around. If there is a leak some-where—and I'm not saying there is—it's better that we should know first."

Wyman couldn't have agreed more.

"I couldn't agree more," he said. "So what are we going to do?"

"This contact of yours in Germany. Are you absolutely sure that he's sound?"

"No. As I said before, he's a mercenary. He'll give information to whomever is waving the most money at him. That's why his price is so high."

"Two million pounds isn't just high. It's outrageous."

"Definitely," Wyman said.

"Are you now absolutely certain there's no other way? I mean, what about our other networks?"

Owen was clutching at straws, and Wyman knew it.

"No one has the quality of contacts that Plato can boast. His intelligence comes straight from the central SED and the detention centres. I explained all this in my original submission."

"Yes, yes." Owen was not happy. "But two million pounds..."

"That two million won't merely buy the information we need. It will also buy Plato's silence. I don't need to tell you that if any of this became known outside the Firm, it would be the worst humiliation since Philby."

"You're right; you don't need to tell me."

Owen's testiness was a sign of capitulation.

"You realize," he said, "that we're creating an appalling precedent."

"It would be an even worse precedent to let a possible leak go unchecked."

Owen sighed.

"You're right, of course. But there's one thing I insist upon. You said in your submission that Plato wanted the money in advance. I can't allow that: he'll get half in advance, and half upon receipt of the goods."

Wyman shook his head.

"He won't accept that."

"He'll have to."

"I think not. I should guess that much of the money is destined to be used in bribes and backhanders for various officials. Plato will need the full sum to keep these officials happy and to cover himself at the same time. I can assure you that he won't be persuaded to take anything less than the full sum, cash in advance."

Owen's face turned purple with rage and frustration.

"For God's sake, who is this man? Doesn't he realize who he's dealing with?"

"I'm afraid he does," Wyman said. "That's why he wants advance payment. We have a very bad reputation about money, you know."

"I must say, you don't seem very bothered by the whole thing."

"I'm not an accountant," Wyman said, "but two million pounds doesn't strike me as being too much to pay for the integrity of the Firm."

Owen groaned in despair and took a couple of indigestion tablets.

"Very well. How does he want to be paid?"

"Via the Swiss bank account which I set up. As soon as the money is paid into it, he will begin his inquiries."

Owen nodded gloomily. One could have been forgiven for supposing that Plato's two million pounds were coming straight from Owen's pocket.

CHAPTER THIRTY-TWO

WYMAN SAT IN HIS MOST COMFORTABLE armchair and watched the nine o'clock news with total indifference. The newsreader's voice calmly and methodically announced the day's catalogue of disasters. Inflation was up by half of one percent, and unemployment was up by 300,000. The Director-General of the CBI expressed his confidence in the Government, and the General Secretary of the TUC reaffirmed his loathing for it.

"A plague on both your houses," Wyman muttered. There was a knock on the door. Wyman got up and opened it. A well-built young man in a Savile Row suit smiled at him and said:

"Dr Wyman? My name is Yuri Tereschkov. May I come in?"

"By all means. Do sit down."

Wyman turned off the television, heedless of the housewife from Bolton, Lancashire, who had just given birth to quintuplets.

"What can I do for you, Mr Tereschkov?"

"I work for the British-Soviet Chamber of Commerce—"

"No," Wyman said genially. "I don't think so."

"No?"

"No," Wyman repeated. "Let me see...you are Captain Anatoli Bulgakov of the KGB. Your face is familiar."

"So." Bulgakov nodded, as if he were conceding a point of debate. "As a matter of fact, I'm a Major now. Your files must be out of date."

"They usually are," Wyman yawned. "Anyway, Major, what can I do for you?"

"It's more a question of what I can do for you. We have received some interesting reports from Rome. You were there recently, I believe."

"That's right. It's very pleasant at this time of year."

"I understand you were inquiring about someone called Josef Grünbaum."

"Actually," Wyman said, "I was in Rome to visit a sick relative in the Trastevere. But do carry on. You're most fascinating, old chap."

"As you know, Grünbaum died recently in unfortunate circumstances."

"Oh dear," Wyman said sympathetically.

"It is rumoured that you have made some very drastic inferences from Grünbaum's death."

"It's the neighbours," Wyman explained. "They do love to gossip."

Bulgakov took a deep breath and continued.

"I heard about your inquiries in Rome, also in Paris and Vienna, and apparently so did the CIA. They have put someone called Rawls onto the case. You know about this, I presume."

"I do now, don't I?"

"I have seen Rawls recently. At our first meeting he tried to kill me—"

"Americans are like that," Wyman observed.

"But we later managed to establish a rapport. He too is a little perplexed by your speculations. We are all anxious to avoid difficulties."

"That's nice."

"There are one or two things you ought to know," Bulgakov said. "Firstly, we have known about Grünbaum for years. To be frank, we never considered him a problem. He did not have access to important information, so we let him carry on with his activities."

"That hardly explains his death."

"His death was a genuine accident. It had nothing to do with us, you must believe that. He had a fight in a bar. When the police arrived to stop the affray, he went berserk. He was shot in self-defence."

"Most reassuring," Wyman said. "May I ask why you are telling me all this?"

Bulgakov smiled.

"I suspect you are planning an investigation into Grünbaum's death. If that is so, you will no doubt send people into Erfurt, and the Americans are sure to follow. That will certainly lead to trouble."

"Indeed. I never really saw the KGB as an organization of trouble-shooters. I will have to revise my opinion of you."

Bulgakov shook his head.

"Naturally, there is more to it than that. There are the arms talks in July. My government is anxious to avoid any scandals that might interfere with the talks. You understand that, I hope."

"I don't know what to understand, Major. Everybody seems to know what is going on in my department, and everybody thinks that it should be stopped. If you were in my position, Major—if you knew the truth of the matter—would you regard that as a deterrent or an incentive to proceed with your plans?"

Bulgakov shrugged.

"I think that you are wasting time and effort on a problem that does not exist. If you proceed, you will create real difficulties for everyone concerned. If operatives are sent into the DDR from your country and America, I will have no option but to stop them. That could be very ugly. Very ugly indeed."

"I'm glad to hear that aesthetics play an important role in your decision-making process, Major."

The smile left Bulgakov's face. He stared coldly at Wyman. "You are facetious, Dr Wyman. I do not think that is appropriate."

"My dear fellow," Wyman protested, "you seem to think you know what we intend to do. You assume that people will be sent into Germany to cause you much discomfort. What are your reasons for assuming that?"

"I have told you. A certain amount can be deduced

from your inquiries in Rome. The misgivings of Rawls complete the picture."

Wyman shook his head.

"Sorry old man, I can't buy that. If Rawls had serious doubts of any sort, he wouldn't tell you about them. He might be American, but he isn't that crass."

"His very presence in London is a sign of what his people think. You have obviously worried them."

"Why, I wonder?"

"You know that better than I do. It can only be because you have asked so many questions about Grünbaum. Worry breeds worry in our profession."

"Yes. A bit like the stock exchange."

"Exactly." Bulgakov smiled again. "Believe me, Grünbaum is not worth worrying about. He was a petty criminal, a small-time gangster with pretensions to greater things. His death signifies nothing."

"How did you find out about him?" Wyman asked. He offered a Rothman to Bulgakov.

"I prefer mine," said Bulgakov. He lit a Dunhill. "Grünbaum? As I said, he was a petty criminal. The *Volkspolizei* found out about his black-market interests, and his other activities soon became known. He received stolen property, sold Western consumer goods at outrageous prices—the usual things. Eventually it became known that he sold information as well. I can't believe that he was of any real use to you. He never had access to interesting information."

Wyman nodded.

"Fascinating," he said. "So what do you suggest we do?"

"Forget about Grünbaum. Call off your investigation."

"It sounds all very cosy," Wyman said. "So all I have to do is say to my people: 'Major Bulgakov dropped in last night. Awfully nice chap. He says we should forget about all this boring Erfurt business.' And if the KGB says everything's all right, it must be, mustn't it?" He smiled benignly.

"I'm sure you can think of something better than that," Bulgakov said.

Wyman scratched his cranium in bewilderment.

"It's all a question of motive, Major. I mean, it's very nice of you to call round and all that, but I have to ask myself what your motives are. Unfortunately, I have to assume that they aren't what you say they are. Nothing personal, you understand."

"Of course."

"It all leads up to one question. You think we're pursuing inquiries in Erfurt. You're trying to dissuade us from doing so. I must therefore conclude that there's something you don't want us to find out. What is it, Major? If you told me that, I really would be persuaded."

Bulgakov laughed quietly.

"I've told you: I don't want any trouble. I don't want to endanger the arms talks in July. That's all."

"We seem to have reached an impasse, Major."

"We do indeed. I have told you everything."

"I rather doubt it," Wyman said. "But you've certainly told me all you're going to tell."

"Yes," Bulgakov said. He put out his cigarette. "And on that note I must leave you, Dr Wyman. Take my advice: don't waste your time on Grünbaum. Good night."

"Cheerio," Wyman said. He showed the major out and returned to his armchair.

"Well, well," he muttered. "How very peculiar."

He poured himself a glass of wine and realized he hadn't offered any to the major. How uncivil of me, he thought.

CHAPTER THIRTY-THREE

"**W**HAT DO WE KNOW ABOUT this Bulgakov fellow?" Owen said.

"Not as much as we'd like," Wyman confessed. "I managed to prise loose the MI5 dossier on him. It's not very substantial, I'm afraid, but it will do for our purposes."

He gave a little cough and consulted his notes.

"Anatoli Vasimovich Bulgakov was born in Minsk in 1947. His father was a war hero. The family moved to Moscow in 1962, and from 1966 to 1969 our friend studied Law at Moscow University. In 1969 Bulgakov was recruited by the First Directorate of the KGB.

"It would seem that Bulgakov is a very bright chap. Thanks to his ability, and his parental connections, he became a favourite of Yuri Andropov, who of course ran the KGB at that time.

"Originally, Bulgakov trained with Department A of the First Directorate—the disinformation crowd. He was also given tuition by the Executive Action Department where, apparently, he graduated with honours."

"So we have a first-class killer on our hands," Owen remarked.

"Indeed," Wyman said. "It would seem that Bulgakov is quite exceptional, even by KGB standards. Clearly, the extent and variety of his tasks imply that he was being groomed for a special position. That position isn't reflected in his rank; apparently he's still only a Major. His importance lies in his ability to function with almost no reference to Moscow Centre. Most of that crowd have to obtain approval from Dzerzhinsky Square before they can do so much as break wind. Not so with our friend Bulgakov: he's completely autonomous."

"What else do we know about him?"

"We first hear of Bulgakov in 1971. At the time he was working for the Second Department in South America—Chile, to be precise.

"The details are somewhat blurred here, but it seems that Bulgakov was helping Allende's government with counterespionage against the CIA, as well as with disinformation and propaganda. When Allende was ousted in late 1973, the military junta expelled Bulgakov, along with every Russian in sight.

"We hear no more of him until 1975 when Bulgakov turned up here in London. Evidently he had been transferred to the Third Department, and they placed him in the British-Soviet Chamber of Commerce."

"What does he do here?"

"A very good question," Wyman said. "The MI5 people are guessing, I think, but this is what they believe. You may recall that in '74 Wilson's Labour Government concluded a trade deal with the USSR, in which the Russians were given a multi-million-pound credit allowance.

"The Russians asked for their own inspectors to be allowed into the factories that were supplying goods to them—Rolls Royce, Ferranti, International Computers, Vickers, Wilkinson Sword, and several others.

"For reasons I still cannot fathom, Wilson and Co. granted that request. Hence the Russians had a golden opportunity to plant KGB men deep into British industry. Needless to say, they took it.

"MI5 think that Bulgakov's job is to supervise and co-ordinate these so-called inspectors. They also think he's responsible for suborning trade union leaders and other people in industry. The point was driven home by the British Security Commission in May '82. Their findings named Bulgakov as a potential security threat.

"But there's no concrete evidence against Bulgakov, and there's no point in sending him home. As far as anyone knows, his role at the Chamber of Commerce is purely administrative, and so he could easily be replaced by somebody else."

"Mmmm." Owen stroked his moustache with an HB pencil. "Do you think that's what Bulgakov is up to?"

"Of course not," Wyman said. "His visit to me last night proves that he's involved in something completely different. Besides, the KGB wouldn't waste someone of

Bulgakov's proven ability by giving him a desk job, would they?"

He lit a cigarette and watched Owen struggle to comprehend all the new information being thrown at him. Owen's perplexity, he noted, was directly proportional to the number of nervous habits Owen displayed. At the moment, Owen's HB pencil was doing the grand tour of Owen's face, his fingers strummed uneasily on Owen's desk, and his rubber-soled shoes shuffled nervously over Owen's nylon carpet.

"What I don't understand, Wyman, is why Bulgakov should visit you in person. What did he think he could gain by it?"

"I should imagine that he wanted to find out what sort of a person I am," Wyman said. "If I turned out to be a cybernetic ice-man like Rawls, Bulgakov might surmise that we were onto something."

"Possibly. And how did you present yourself, out of interest?"

"It was getting late," Wyman smiled. "I tend to become a little vague at that time of day."

"It doesn't make sense," Owen said. "Doesn't the man realize that by warning us off he's simply inviting us to go in? Perhaps he wants us to go in."

"Perhaps. He mentioned the Geneva arms talks, but I don't think he's particularly bothered about them one way or the other. It has occurred to me, however, that he might be setting up some sort of trap."

"A trap? What do you mean?"

"It's a little involved," Wyman said, "But please be patient. Bulgakov assured me that anyone we sent into the DDR would be immediately picked up. The fact is, the KGB know very little about how we get people in and out of the satellite states. We're actually quite good at it. It's one of the few areas in which we are notably more successful than the Americans; for some reason, the Company's failure rate in infiltration is very high."

"So?"

"So just suppose we did send someone in. If Bulgakov does have a ferret working here, the whole procedure could be reported back to him in detail. Bulgakov could grab our man, and he would also learn about our infiltration system. Hence, it's to Bulgakov's advantage that we send someone in.

"On the other hand, if we don't send someone in, if we just sit back and forget about the whole thing as Bulgakov suggests, then our KGB ferret will remain happily undetected. Either way suits Bulgakov fine."

"This assumes, of course, that someone here really is a KGB plant."

"Of course. But I think we must assume that."

"Why?"

"Because none of this would have arisen had it not been for our suspicions regarding Grünbaum's demise. Anyway, the plot thickens here. It would seem that we have two alternative courses of action, and both of them are to Bulgakov's advantage. Either we send someone in, and Bulgakov grabs them, or we ignore the whole thing, and Bulgakov's ferret lives happily ever after. This is the situation Bulgakov presented me with, and that, I think, is why he visited me in person."

"I still don't understand," Owen said.

"Please bear with me," Wyman said. "Bulgakov is a realist, is he not? He knows that we suspect a plant, and he knows that unless he's careful, we'll find out who that plant is. Therefore, the best thing, from his point of view, would be for us to abandon the search. But as I say, he's a realist. He can't conceive that we might give up the hunt for the sake of a few pennies."

"There's no need to be snide," Owen said.

"It's the truth, isn't it? Could Bulgakov really conceive of that happening? Of course not. So Bulgakov must assume that we will pursue inquiries. And if we must conduct an inquiry, Bulgakov would like us to do it in the way that suits him best, namely, by sending a man into Germany.

"And so he posits the two alternatives as if they're the only two, and that's what he wants us to believe. But of course they aren't. We don't need to send people into Germany: we could make exhaustive internal inquiries, or, better still, we could use a contact like Plato. That sort of thing must worry Bulgakov enormously."

"I see," Owen said. "An incredibly tortuous piece of reasoning, but I take your point. Nevertheless, you're making one big assumption here."

"What's that?"

"You assume that Bulgakov's mind is as complex and duplicitous as the average don's."

"The Russians do produce good chess players," Wyman said.

"It doesn't occur to you that Bulgakov might have been telling the truth? That he really does want to avert a scandal? That Grünbaum really was a nobody? And, by implication, that there is no Soviet plant in this department?"

"It has occurred to me," Wyman said. "But I'm not inclined to take the words of a KGB officer at their face value. If KGB men spoke the truth, people like us would be out of a job, wouldn't we?"

Owen coughed in embarrassment.

CHAPTER THIRTY-FOUR

ON THE AFTERNOON OF MAY 28, Rawls flew to Schönefeld airport in Berlin. There he changed onto an *Interflug* service, and he arrived at Erfurt shortly afterwards. He was travelling as Thompson Clarke, an American businessman specializing in the buying and selling of flowers.

Rawls had chosen his cover well: the *Internationale Gartenbauausstellung*, Erfurt's horticultural show, spans 250 acres and is open all the year round. It attracts specialists and dealers from all over the world, and provides an excellent cover for the traveller who is clearly no tourist.

A taxi took Rawls to the vast new Interhotel Kosmos on the Krämpferstrasse. The Kosmos is a luxurious four-star megalith in the very heart of Erfurt, and it suited Rawls' needs admirably. He was shown to a

174

room on the twelfth floor, and after a quick shower and shave he persuaded the restaurant staff to give him an early meal. The evening menu had not yet been prepared, so Rawls had to content himself with a cold plate of *Thüringer Kesselfleisch,* one of the local sausage dishes.

Having finished his meal, Rawls left the hotel and went for an early evening stroll. He walked through the Anger Boulevard, Erfurt's main shopping street, and passed by the heavy grey-brown Kaufmann church, where Luther said mass in 1522. He then turned into Hermann-Jahn Strasse and crossed over the river Gera.

Had he bothered to look over to the right, Rawls would have seen the brightly coloured Krämerbrücke or Grocer's Bridge, one of Erfurt's main tourist attractions. The bridge dates back to 1325 and consists of a row of three-storey houses painted red, yellow and white stretching right across the river, held above the water by wooden rafters and brick columns. But Rawls did not bother to look to the right, and he would have ignored the bridge even if he had seen it.

Once he was over the river, Rawls walked down to the end of Hermann-Jahn Strasse, and turned left into a maze of narrow side-streets. He consulted his pocket-map and walked around until he found a small bar called Der Satz. He entered it and saw that there were no customers.

A plump little barman with no hair and the complexion of a dead fish was drying some beer glasses behind the bar.

"I'm afraid we're closed," the barman said.

"I'm glad to hear it," Rawls said. "I'd like a beer, please."

The barman's expression did not change. His little blue eyes gazed calmly at Rawls as he continued to dry the glasses.

"What beer would you like?" he asked.

"Do you serve American beers? Pabst, Michelob, anything like that?"

"You come to Germany and ask for American beer? That's a little strange, isn't it?"

"I get homesick, Herr Schlick."

The barman went over to the door and locked it. He then drew the blinds down over the entrance and returned to the bar, where he pulled out two bottles and opened them.

"You can't get American beer in this country," he said. "Welcome to Erfurt, Mr Rawls."

"Thank you," Rawls said. He took a large mouthful of the cold amber lager and sat down on a stool.

"What can I do for you?" Herr Schlick said.

"Didn't they tell you?"

"Tell me again."

"Still not convinced?" Rawls grinned.

"Certain convictions can be very costly in the DDR, Mr Rawls."

"Okay. I want to find out about Neumann, and, if possible, to meet him. Can that be arranged?"

"Perhaps, but it won't be easy. Nobody knows anything about Neumann, and his present condition is anybody's guess."

"You mean he could be dead?"

"It's possible. All we know for certain is that if he's alive, he's definitely in the hospital."

"Can I get in there?"

"Very difficult," said Schlick. He wiped a finger across his chin to remove a small dribble of lager. He licked the finger pensively and gazed down at his glass. "You can imagine what kind of a place it is. Heavily guarded."

"So what do I do?"

Schlick smiled thinly.

"If I were you, I'd go home," he said. "I don't know what you're after, but it can't be worth this sort of trouble."

"I'll be the judge of that."

"Judge, jury and executioner," Schlick observed. "Very well. We once managed to get somebody in there. His motives were no doubt less worthy than yours: he wanted to steal some drugs. But the basic difficulty was the same."

"What did you do?"

"One of the doctors at the hospital is having an affair with a local girl. He usually calls round at her place for a quickie while he's supposed to be on the early evening shift. His movements are easy to time because she doesn't get home from work until quarter to six, and he can only be absent from work between half-five and seven. Before then the afternoon staff would notice his absence, and the night staff are all there by seven o'clock. So, allowing for driving time, we can usually count on him turning up at about six o'clock and leaving half an hour later."

"That's definitely a quickie. What does this do for me?"

"The doctor drives a clapped-out old Trabant. I'll give you the registration number. When nobody's looking, it's very easy to open the boot and climb in—you know how to do such things?"

"Yes," Rawls said.

"Good. The Trabant boot is easier to open than most. If you can manage that, the rest should be quite straightforward. Just wait until the good doctor has finished his lovemaking, and he will drive you right into the hospital."

"How about getting out of the place?"

"The doctor finishes his shift at about eight-thirty. If you haven't got what you want by then, you will have to hide until the morning and repeat the performance with one of the night-workers' cars. Remember, the whole building is heavily patrolled. Don't even contemplate breaking out of it—that would be far too dangerous."

Schlick pulled out a small notepad and wrote some details on it. He then tore the page out and handed it to Rawls.

"This is the girl's address. You have a map? Good. The number below it is the registration number of the doctor's car. Be there between five to six and half past. If he doesn't turn up, try again the next evening."

"Thanks," Rawls said, pocketing the note. "Tell me, what exactly is this place? Is it really a hospital?"

"Oh yes," Schlick said. "It contains genuine, old-fashioned lunatics. They also throw in the occasional political criminal, but it's principally a madhouse. The man you want: he's a political offender, I suppose?"

"Something like that," Rawls said.

"He must be very important to you to merit all this trouble."

"He is. I think he knows something vital."

"Really?" Schlick sounded almost impressed.

"Listen," Rawls said. "Has there been any police or military activity around here lately? Unusual activity, I mean?"

"Not that I know of," Schlick said. "In fact it's been very quiet."

"What about Grünbaum? Why was he arrested?"

"Who knows?" Schlick said, but his eyes twinkled. "I had nothing to do with Grünbaum. He was a criminal. Dangerous company."

"He never did any work for us?"

"America? No. There was some talk of him working for the West, but it was probably just rumour."

"These rumours, where did they come from?"

"People," Schlick smiled. "Just people. You must understand, there were many stories told about Grünbaum. He was a gangster. People like to invent stories about such people. Myths."

"I see," Rawls said, but he was not convinced. "Do you know anyone who knew him? Someone I could talk to."

"Let me see..." Schlick tilted back his head and thought about it for a moment. "There was someone. A man called Carnap. I have occasional dealings with him. He may be able to help."

"Can I see him?"

"Perhaps. I will try to arrange it if you like. Come back and see me when you have finished your business at the hospital. If you finish it."

Rawls drained his glass of beer and produced a thick manila envelope from his jacket.

"I think you'll find it's all here," he said.

"Excellent," Schlick said. "You'd never imagine how useful Western currency is in these parts."

"I've got a pretty good imagination," Rawls said. "It goes with the job. See you in a couple of days."

He left the bar and returned to the hotel.

CHAPTER THIRTY-FIVE

WYMAN SAT ON MARGARET'S SOFA in Margaret's fiat, immersed in brandy, Margaret and Chopin's Nocturne number 3. She lay across the sofa, dozing with her head in his lap, oblivious to the music and the worries in Wyman's mind.

He blew out a long stream of cigarette smoke and looked at his watch. It was 2.20 A.M.

"It's two-twenty," he said.

"Mmmm," Margaret said.

"The house is on fire."

"Mmmm."

"World War Three has just been declared."

"Who cares?"

"I'm going to have a baby."

"That isn't funny," she giggled.

"No," he said.

She opened her eyes and looked up at him.

"Are you all right?" she asked.

"I'm going to have to go away."

"Where?"

"Europe again. It's my last job."

She frowned.

"What's happening? I don't understand."

He sighed and put out his cigarette.

"I'm supposed to negotiate a transaction with someone in Germany. After that I shall leave the Firm."

"Do they know?"

"They will."

There was a pause as the nocturne rippled to a close.

"How long will you be?"

"Only a few days."

"What about me?"

Wyman smiled and stroked her hair gently.

"That's the six thousand dollar question."

"And what's the six thousand dollar answer?"

He removed his glasses and reached for his cigarettes. He pulled out two, lit them, and put one in Margaret's mouth.

"If I asked you to live with me in Europe, would you find the idea utterly horrendous?"

"No, of course not," she said. "Why do you want to go? I thought you were the great patriot."

"I was. I still am. But it's going to be very difficult to get used to England without the College and the Firm. Especially the College."

She smiled.

"I can never understand your feelings for that university," she said. "All that back-stabbing and one-upmanship. And they haven't exactly repaid your loyalty, have they?"

He sipped his brandy and felt its warm silky vapour brush gently past his taste-buds and down his throat.

"The College is far more than the sum of the people who run it at any one time. If the present incumbents have no use for me, that is no reflection on the College itself. That may sound corny and metaphysical, but I believe it. Besides, I can't exactly blame the College Council for my present misfortune. They have their own difficulties, you know. Everyone's being hit by the recession nowadays."

"Loyal to the last," she said.

"Yes."

"I don't understand," she said. "The Conservatives are supposed to be the Establishment party. You're an Establishment figure if ever there was one. You should be the last person to suffer from Government policy. It doesn't make sense."

"The flaw," Wyman said in his most scholarly tone, "lies in your major premise. The Conservatives *were* the Establishment party. They aren't any longer."

"Major premise," she said mockingly. "I'm not an undergraduate any more, you know."

"And I'm not a don any more, but you take my point. Oxbridge logicians are no longer Downing Street's flavour of the month."

"Yes," she conceded. "But why don't you get a job teaching at another university? Just because the College doesn't want you—"

"You think I should work in some redbrick, do

you?" Wyman snorted. "A tremendous idea. I can just picture myself sitting happily in a plastic-and-chrome lecturers' common room in some squalid provincial city, exchanging pleasantries with sociologists with halitosis, structuralists with dyed hair and earrings, and the entire panoply of middle-class Marxists. A fitting end to a distinguished academic career, don't you think?"

Margaret laughed.

"Michael, you're a snob."

"Possibly," he said. "But that doesn't alter the fact that I would be desperately unhappy in such an environment."

"I suppose so," she said. "But the redbricks aren't the only alternative. What about universities abroad? Harvard? Heidelberg? Bologna? The Sorbonne?"

"Yes, yes, I've thought about it, and it's an interesting idea. The question is, would they take a logician with my background? That remains to be seen. It's part of the reason why I'd like to move abroad."

"And I'm to come with you?"

"If you want."

"I want," she said. "Where do you have in mind?"

"I don't know yet. What I intend is to go to Europe for this last chore for the Firm, and I simply won't return. I'll find us a place, send you the address, and we'll meet there. How does that sound?"

"How am I supposed to meet you? I can barely afford a bus fare nowadays, let alone a plane ticket."

"I'll put some money into your account."

Her eyes narrowed in suspicion.

"You've thought it all out, haven't you?"

He nodded.

"There's one more thing," he said.

"Go on."

"I don't want the Firm to hear about what we're doing. My final wages will be paid on the thirtieth, and they are based upon my retiring at the end of June. In fact, I will have severed my links with the Firm by the first week of June, if not earlier. Hence, I'd rather the Firm knew nothing about my movements until after the money has been paid."

"Are they really that mean with money?"

"Intolerably niggardly. Owen has become obsessed with savings; I think he's under pressure from the Minister."

"It's ridiculous," she said. "You can't run an intelligence department on the cheap, especially yours."

"I know that and you know that," Wyman said. "And even Owen knows that, though he won't admit it. Unfortunately, the powers that be don't know that. Hence I am out of work."

He drained his glass of brandy.

"What I propose to do is send you a postcard from wherever I'll be, simply signed 'Betty'. There'll be an address on it, and when you receive it, meet me there."

"Yes, master," she said. "This is all a bit cloak and dagger, isn't it?"

"For a month's wages," he said, "I am prepared to understudy Cesare Borgia."

CHAPTER THIRTY-SIX

"**D**ESCRIBE HIM TO ME," Bulgakov said.

"Tall, well-built. Late thirties. Short dark hair. Wears steel-rimmed tinted glasses. Quietly dressed. Travels light."

Captain Fichte read from his notes.

"Rawls," Bulgakov said. "It has to be. What does his shoe say?"

"His passport gives the name Thompson Clarke. He claims to be a flower salesman."

Bulgakov grinned.

"Clearly Mr Rawls does have a sense of humour, despite all appearances."

"We get many such people coming to Erfurt, Herr Major. The International Flower Show—"

"I know, I know," Bulgakov snapped impatiently. "Did you follow him?"

"He's staying at the Interhotel Kosmos, Herr Major."

"Don't put a tail on him," Bulgakov said thoughtfully. "He'd spot that at once. Just keep an eye on the hotel."

"What are you going to do, Herr Major?"

"For the time being, nothing. Try to get a photograph of him as he leaves the hotel, but do be discreet."

"Of course, Herr Major," Fichte said, deeply shocked that the major should regard him capable of an indiscretion.

"Is his phone tapped?"

"All the telephones in the hotel are tapped."

"Yes," Bulgakov said. "He'll expect that, I suppose." His eyes narrowed in concentration.

"He'll have to move about in public, especially if he's posing as a businessman. Very well, once you have the photograph, circulate it among the police at the railway station and bus depots, as well as the car-hire centre. Emphasize that he is not to be apprehended or detained. Tell them to let us know whenever he is spotted. For the time being, I simply wish to keep an eye on his movements."

"Is he a dangerous man, Herr Major?"

"He eats your sort for breakfast," Bulgakov growled, noting with satisfaction the look of horror on Fichte's face.

"Do we know what he's going to do?"

"I don't think even he knows, Hauptmann. With the Americans strategy is all and tactics are ignored."

"You seem to have personal knowledge of this man."

"I have," Bulgakov said. "We first met in Chile about ten years ago. In those days, things were going entirely his way. I suspect the positions are now reversed."

"I presume he will be shot, Herr Major?"

"Don't presume anything, Hauptmann," Bulgakov smiled. "After all, he might shoot you."

Fichte paled.

"Will that be all, Herr Major?"

"Yes, for now. Thank you, Hauptmann."

Fichte left the office.

"Prick," said Bulgakov, in Russian.

CHAPTER THIRTY-SEVEN

WYMAN FLEW FROM LONDON to Geneva on the morning of May 30. Once again, he travelled under the assumed name of Edmund Ryle. The Banque Internationale Descartes greeted him with its customary deference, and when he explained that he wished to deposit some cash into a numbered account, he was escorted to the office of M. Barthes.

Barthes was a little taken aback at being presented with two million pounds sterling in used fifty-pound notes, but he was not unduly upset about it. With a couple of assistants, he counted the notes and satisfied himself that everything was in order. He then produced a form which Wyman filled in and signed, certifying that the two million had been paid into account G2H-17-493 on that date. Barthes then gave Wyman a receipt for the money, and the two men shook hands.

Wyman then asked if it would be possible to have a quick word with M. Piaget, the manager. Barthes assured Wyman that Piaget would be delighted to see him. Under the circumstances, Wyman was not particularly surprised.

Piaget received Wyman with all the geniality and blandishment that he reserved for the wealthiest of clients. It occurred to Wyman that whereas people in his own profession regarded insincerity as a tool of their trade, people like M. Piaget had turned it into an artform.

Wyman ignored Piaget's outpourings and got straight to the point. He had a rather extraordinary request to make, but he felt it was in the interest of both his client and the bank that M. Piaget should grant it. He explained the nature of his request, and M. Piaget assured him that it would be no trouble at all. Wyman thanked M. Piaget for his consideration, and he left the manager's office.

As he stepped out of the bank, Wyman noticed a group of workmen on the other side of the road. One of them stood behind what looked vaguely like a theodolite. Wyman noticed that there were no road-works in progress, and that the theodolite was pointed directly at the entrance to the bank.

He went over to the workmen and smiled at them graciously.

"Good morning, gentlemen," he said in English. "And how is life in the Company nowadays?"

The workmen stared at him blankly. The man behind the theodolite said:

"Who the fuck are you?"

"I'm the chap you're looking for. Consult your photograph, if you want to make sure."

The theodolite man looked at one of his colleagues, and the other man nodded.

"That is a camera, isn't it?" Wyman said. "Thought so. We used to use those things as well, but we gave up on them. The telephoto lens is too conspicuous, you see."

The theodolite man scratched his head in bewilderment.

"You know who we are?"

"Of course I do," Wyman said cheerfully.

"I'm confused," one of the workmen said.

"It's a common problem," Wyman observed. "Look here, since I'm the one you're after, why not take a decent photo of me now? Once you've done that, you can go home."

"You want us to take your picture?" The theodolite man was totally perplexed.

"Yes, why not?" Wyman said. "I'm always ready to oblige my American colleagues. You'll find that the right is my best side, but I suppose you want the entire face."

"Yeah," gasped the theodolite man. "The whole face—if you don't mind, sir."

By now the "workmen" were convinced that they were dealing with a raving lunatic.

"Splendid." Wyman beamed genially at the camera as the theodolite man took the photograph. "Better take another one, just to make sure."

The theodolite man took another photo and looked up at Wyman.

"Thank you, sir," he said.

"Not at all," Wyman said. "Good morning."

"Good morning," said the workmen.

Wyman strolled away to find a taxi.

CHAPTER THIRTY-EIGHT

WHILE MICHAEL WYMAN WAS sorting out Plato's finances in Geneva, Rawls wandered around the luxuriant gardens of the International Flower Show in Erfurt. Rawls was not sure if his movements were being noted, so he felt obliged to pay at least one visit to the show, to validate the claims on his visa.

The colourful displays and pretty fountains bored Rawls, so he lingered at the show only for as long as was absolutely necessary. He then headed back towards the hotel, swearing that he would never look at another flower again. On the way home he paid a brief visit to the thirteenth-century monastery on the Augustinierstrasse, and then he walked down the Leninstrasse to the Interhotel Kosmos.

At the hotel Rawls took a late lunch, and sampled some more of the local cuisine. Although he was no epicure, Rawls could appreciate a good meal, and lunch at the Kosmos did not disappoint him. Thuringia specializes in venison, poultry and fish, and along with its fine range of sausage dishes it produces a very fine ham known as *Bärenschinken*. Feeling a little spoilt for choice, Rawls decided to save these delights for another occasion. He settled for another local dish, *Thüringer Sauerkrauten mit Klössen* (pickled roast meat with dumplings) which he washed down with a bottle of Bulgarian wine.

After lunch Rawls had a look at the hotel's Intershop. Intershops are an indication of the strange nature of the East German economy. The official exchange rate of the West German and East German marks is one to one, but since 1949 the East Germans have been prepared to offer four to five DDR marks for one West German mark.

This is not to say that everything is more expensive in the East: rents, fares, gas, electricity, bread and butter actually cost less in the DDR. But cars, electrical goods, clothing, shoes, confectionery and fruit are more expensive, so by taking their own marks into the DDR, West Germans could eat in East German restaurants and buy consumer items at virtually no cost. With the increase in West German visitors in recent years, the black market in currency and consumer goods thrived, as did the careers of people like Josef Grünbaum.

In order to cope with this problem, as well as the desperate need for Western currency, Intershops were established throughout the DDR in 1962. Originally, these were solely for the benefit of tourists; they sold Western goods for Western currency, and the East

Germans themselves were not allowed to use them. Naturally, the East Germans broke the law, and in 1974 the Intershops were officially made available to the East German public.

Nevertheless, the DDR's government still maintains its ambivalent attitude towards them. To the Westerner, the Intershops are oddly reminiscent of the Soho sex-shop. No window displays are allowed and, once inside the shop, the customer is given the impression that he is being given access to something suspect and slightly naughty.

The Intershops had never provided an effective opposition to black-marketeers like Grünbaum, and they did very little for Western visitors. Rawls was not impressed by the goods on sale in the Kosmos Intershop. The quality of the items was slightly inferior to those on sale in the average Woolworth's, and Rawls had no inclination to waste his money on them. He left the shop and sat in the main lounge of the hotel, drinking coffee.

Rawls read the notepaper given him by Schlick. The address he sought was Number 39, Dorfstrasse. He consulted his map and established that this street lay in the newly built housing estate surrounding the Nordhäuser Strasse in the north of Erfurt. He guessed it would take him about three-quarters of an hour to walk there. He considered hiring a car, but decided that this might attract unwanted attention. So at ten past five he left the hotel and walked northwards up the Juri-Gagarin Ring.

The walk took a little longer than he had expected, and he finally arrived at Dorfstrasse at 6.10. He found

Number 39, and noted that there was no car outside.
That would mean loitering, but in that respect Rawls was
fortunate. The Nordhäuser district is unusual among
East German housing estates in that its planners were
prepared to take aesthetic considerations into account
when designing it. Opposite the block of houses was a
large fountain surrounded by well-tended gardens. Rawls
sat down on a bench near the fountain and kept an eye
on Number 39. He was delighted to see that the street
was empty, and prayed that it would remain so.

At 6.22 a rusty old saloon car stopped outside the
house, and its driver got out. Rawls read the number
plate, confirming that this was the car he wanted. The
driver locked the car and rang the doorbell of Number
39. Eight seconds later the door opened, and the man
was shown inside by a young woman. The door shut,
and four seconds after that the front curtains were
drawn. Rawls wondered if they were planning to do it in
the front room, and realized that he would have to be
especially careful not to make any noise.

He crept swiftly over to the car and tried the boot.
Not surprisingly, it was locked. He drew out a small
lock-pick from his breast pocket and carefully opened
the boot. Inside was an empty petrol can, a few rags and
a spanner. He moved these aside and climbed in. Having
satisfied himself that he would be secure and comfortable, he attached a strip of insulating tape across the
lock and then shut himself inside the boot. So far, everything was proceeding according to plan.

Twenty minutes later, Dr Johannes Leibniz emerged
from Number 39. He had the flushed, contented look of
a man who has just enjoyed illicit sex. A quick glance at

the street assured him that no one was about, and he returned to his car.

As he started the engine, Leibniz wondered if he might not be getting too old for this sort of thing. The girl was very pneumatic. Still, it compensated for what his wife Hilde failed to provide. When it came to love-making, Hilde had all the imagination and stamina one could expect of a geriatric walrus.

He drove back towards the hospital and looked at his watch. It was now 7.10, and he was slightly late. Unfortunately, the car was handling very sluggishly at the moment, and that would probably account for the delay. He must remember to have the car seen to tomorrow; it was probably just the tyres. The delay meant that he would have to do his rounds a little more briskly than usual before finishing his paperwork and going home to Hilde. It wasn't a particularly stimulating agenda, but Leibniz had had enough stimulation for one day.

He pulled up at the gates of a grey building-complex on the outskirts of Mühlhausen. A large sign said "Heisenberg Psychiatric Institute". A guard approached the car and Leibniz lowered his window. He waved his pass at the guard.

"Good evening, Sergeant," he said.

"Good evening, Dr Leibniz," the guard said, grinning evilly. "Did you have a pleasant ride?"

"Most pleasant, thank you," Leibniz said uncomfortably. He wondered who had been talking.

The guard waved to a colleague, and the gates opened. The saloon rolled down a long gravel drive and halted among a group of similar cars. Leibniz got out of his car and went into the hospital.

A minute later, Rawls partially opened the boot of the car and looked around. Nobody was in sight. He jumped out, tore off the insulating tape, and closed the boot. He looked at the main entrance to the hospital, took a deep breath, and walked inside.

To Rawls' intense relief, the receptionist's desk was unattended. He saw a corridor plan of the building pinned up against a wall. It told him that the Records Department was in room F37 on the fourth floor.

A large clock on the wall read 7.28. It was still too early, Rawls decided. He looked at the chart and saw that the laundry was to be found in the basement. He walked over to a flight of stairs and went down.

He hid in the laundry, and after three hours his patience was exhausted. He donned a white porter's jacket and walked out into the neon-lit corridor. A couple of nurses passed by without noticing him.

It took him five minutes to find room F37. He was disgusted to see that it was still lit. Through the glass door he could see a night porter reading a magazine. Evidently, the Records Office had the best coffee in the building. He walked in and said hello to the porter.

"Hello," said the porter, without looking up.

"I wonder if you can help me," Rawls said. "I'm new here. Dr Leibniz asked me to get him a file on somebody called Kurt Neumann."

"Over there." The porter waved laconically at a row of filing cabinets by the window. "They're in alphabetical order. I thought Leibniz had gone home."

"He has," Rawls said. "He told me to put it on his desk for the morning."

"Morning?" The porter's eyes widened in surprise.

"So he's doing morning shifts as well now, is he? The man's a workaholic."

"Yes," Rawls said.

He walked over to the filing cabinets and found the one containing Neumann's papers. He took the file out, thanked the porter, and left the room. A couple of minutes later he was back in the laundry.

He read quickly through the documents. They were very surprising. Rawls frowned in confusion and sat down.

"What the fuck is going on?" he muttered. "Doesn't make sense."

He reread the file for further clues, but could find none. He noted that Neumann was in a single ward on the second floor.

Beneath a sink at the other end of the laundry was a waste-disposal unit. Rawls shoved the documents into the hatch and walked out.

Neumann's room was unlocked and unlit. Rawls switched on a small table-lamp and saw a bulky figure asleep on the bed.

"Neumann, wake up."

Neumann grunted and opened one eye. He was a large, muscular man in his late forties.

"Who are you?" he said.

"A friend," Rawls said. "You must be very quiet."

"Why?"

"Because I'm not supposed to be here. I'm from the Company."

"Is this a game?" Neumann said. "I like games."

"I need some information," Rawls said. "Who blew Grünbaum? How were you busted?"

"Shall I call a nurse? Maybe she'd like to play too."

"Listen!" Rawls hissed. "This is important: you've got to tell me how your network was discovered. What happened?"

"I don't understand," Neumann said.

"What I mean is, how did you get here?"

"Oh, that," Neumann said. "That was all because of Auntie Gretchen."

"Who? Is that a code-name?"

"Auntie Gretchen. I lived with her," Neumann explained. "She was very kind, even though she beat me sometimes."

"What the hell are you talking about?" Rawls said.

"She said that if I wasn't good, the men would take me away. That's what they do to all the bad children. 'But I'm not bad, Auntie', I said."

"Jesus Christ!" Rawls exclaimed.

"Anyway," Neumann continued, "I was chopping wood for Auntie Gretchen, and she came out and started shouting at me."

"Why the fuck did she shout at you?"

"Because she never asked me to chop the wood. She was very angry, and I was only trying to be good."

"Sure," Rawls groaned. "I bet you're a regular sweetie."

"She shouted at me so much I had to make her stop. So I hit her with the axe."

"You did what?"

"I hit her. Not very hard. Just a few times on her head to stop her shouting."

"What happened?"

"She stopped shouting."

"No, I mean what happened to you?"

"The men came and took me away. They say I can't see Auntie Gretchen any more. I want to go home, but they won't let me."

Neumann started to blub.

"That's really very sad," Rawls said, though he didn't put much feeling into it. "Listen Neumann, I've got one more question to ask. Just one, and then I'll go away."

Neumann sniffed and nodded.

"Neumann—Kurt—how old are you? Can you tell me that? What is your age?"

Neumann frowned in concentration.

"I'm a big boy now," he said.

"I can see that," Rawls said. "But how old are you?"

"I'm older than Eva, I know that."

"And how old is Eva?"

"Eva's nine," Neumann said. "Do you want to meet Eva?"

He picked up a small, mangled teddy bear and showed it to Rawls.

"Eva's my best friend," he said proudly.

Rawls nodded.

"Yeah," he said. "Well, I'll be seeing you."

He put the light out and left the room.

Rawls walked down the stairs and into the main entrance hall. It was still empty. He went over to the door and opened it. He stepped outside and doubled up in pain as a rifle-butt hit him in the stomach. He fell to the ground and saw a guard swing the rifle-butt upwards.

It all happened in a second and it saved Rawls' life. His left leg hooked around the guard's ankle while his right foot drove straight into the guard's kneecap and smashed it. As the guard fell backwards, Rawls dived onto him and shoved a flattened palm into his windpipe, shattering the larynx.

Whether the guard would die of internal bleeding or suffocation Rawls did not particularly care. He leapt over him and ran outside. People were shouting on all sides. There were whistles, and he thought he could make out the bark of a dog. He rushed towards the parked cars. As he got to the nearest one he groped in his pocket for the lock-pick. Just as the boot came open, Rawls' world exploded into a kaleidoscope of red, gold, brown and finally black.

CHAPTER THIRTY-NINE

A BRIGHTLY LIT CELL CAME gradually into focus, and Rawls felt a herd of distressed elephants stampede across his cranium. From the corner of his eye he could see a bucket on the floor. He leaned over and threw up into it. This did not make him feel better, but at least it was something to do.

He sat up and blinked at the man opposite. "I did warn you," Bulgakov said.

"You were very kind," Rawls said weakly. "I'll remember you at Christmas."

Bulgakov grinned and offered Rawls a cigarette. Rawls shook his head.

"So now you know," Bulgakov said.

"Yeah."

"Was it worth the trouble? Was it really worth it?"
Rawls shrugged.

"We had to know."

"You could have spared yourself all this discomfort simply by believing what I said."

"Listen, Bulgakov, I'm not self-employed. Even if I believed you, my boss wouldn't. I'd still have had to come here."

"Perhaps."

There was a short silence, and then Rawls said:

"What have you got lined up for me?"

"I could kill you," Bulgakov said thoughtfully. "After all, you killed that guard."

"You don't look too bothered about that."

"I'm not. I regard your life as slightly more important than that of some German fool. Besides, killing you would be silly."

"I'm glad you think so," Rawls said.

"If you died, more people would follow you. Your people would think that you had discovered something important."

"So?"

"So I shall send you home. You can tell your masters—and the British—about what you have seen. That, I hope, will be the end of the matter."

Rawls nodded. There was very little to say.

CHAPTER FORTY

NAGEL SAT IN HIS OFFICE and ate a pizza which Miss Langer had sent up. As usual, just as much food went onto Nagel's clothes and carpet as went into his mouth. A large pile of reports sat on Nagel's desk, but Nagel was not disposed to go through it. Instead, he watched a video of the last World Series. It was so much more entertaining.

The intercom buzzed and Nagel answered it.

"Yeah?" he grunted elegantly.

"Mr Nagel? A couple of photographs have just arrived from Geneva, and we've got the Geneva people on the line. Will you take the call?"

"Yeah, all right. Send the photos up."

There was a click on the intercom, and a distant voice came through.

"Hello, Mr Nagel?"

"Yeah, that's me."

"This is Dwight Davidson in Geneva. We got the photos of Wyman at the Banque Descartes."

"Well?"

"I thought I ought to explain. Apparently, Wyman was expecting them there."

"Expecting them? What do you mean?"

"Our people were rigged up as workmen, and the camera was a phony theodolite. Wyman saw them, and just walked up and said hello."

Nagel stared incredulously at the intercom.

"Is this some kind of sick joke?"

"No sir, it's the truth. He just walked up, said he knew who they were and invited them to take a close-up shot."

"It's impossible," Nagel said. "How the fuck could—?"

"I don't know, sir. We were as amazed as you are, and you can guess how the guys felt about it."

"You sure it's Wyman?"

"Positive, sir. Look at the photographs."

"Hold on," Nagel said. In a voice that could be heard across most of Virginia, he bawled:

"Miss Langer! Where are those fucking photographs?"

"Coming sir," said a voice in the corridor.

The world-weary Miss Langer trotted into the office and put the photographs on Nagel's desk. Nagel gave a snort of thanks, and stared at the pictures.

"Jesus H. Christ!" he exclaimed.

Both prints clearly displayed Wyman's grinning cherubic features.

"You're right, Davidson," Nagel said. "It is Wyman."

"Good. I thought you'd want to know."

"Yeah, thanks."

Nagel rang off and examined the prints. How Wyman could have known that the CIA were looking out for him was a mystery to Nagel. Matters were not helped by the look of impudent glee plastered across Wyman's face in the photographs.

"What the fuck is that bastard up to?" Nagel muttered.

He wrote a message on his notepad for Rawls: TO RAWLS 0236C. PLATO JUST WON THE SWEEPSTAKES. WYMAN IN GENEVA ON 30/5. NAGEL.

He then pushed the intercom button and spoke to Miss Langer.

"Listen," he said, "I've got a message for Rawls. Send it to the Company offices at US embassies in Bonn, Paris, London, Berne, Rome, Berlin, Copenhagen and Madrid. I don't know where he is, but if he doesn't get the message it's his own fuckin' fault."

He read the message out and switched off the intercom. It occurred to Nagel that if Plato had now been paid, Wyman might well know the identity of the infiltrator in MI6. Either that, or Plato was being paid in advance. If that was the case, it would not be long before the ferret would be rooted out.

Nagel fervently hoped that Rawls had accomplished his mission in Europe. If he had not, the consequences could involve a major public embarrassment for MI6 at a time when both the British and the Americans least required it.

He looked once more at the photographs of Wyman. The pictures indicated the genial nincompoop that everyone assumed Wyman to be. It began to dawn upon Nagel that Wyman had been playing on that assumption. But to what end?

CHAPTER FORTY-ONE

IT WAS 11.30 P.M. THE BEST THAT the Minister's Club could manage at this late hour was a snack of smoked salmon and a chilled bottle of Meursault 1959.

"Any word from Wyman?" asked the Minister.

"None yet," Owen said.

"When do you expect to hear from him?"

"Soon. The minute he gets what he needs from Plato, he'll return to London. With a bit of luck we'll have the ferret behind bars without delay."

"We'd better," the Minister said. "I've had a great deal of trouble justifying the expense to the PM. If Wyman doesn't produce, we're all in trouble."

"I know," Owen said. "Wyman's a good man. I'm sure he'll manage it."

"Bloody dons," said the Minister. "I never liked 'em.

Too damned clever for everybody's good. And they expect everyone else to be the same."

The Minister had just managed a third in Land Economy at Cambridge. His memories of those who had taught him were not fond ones.

"Wyman is a typical example," he continued. "Spends other people's money as if there's no tomorrow. Dons are like that. They live too damned well, that's what it's all about. They sit in the lap of collegiate luxury like medieval barons, and when you pull them out into the real world they expect to carry on as usual. They're out of date, Owen, completely out of date."

He nibbled vehemently at his smoked salmon.

"It's Plato who wants the two million, not Wyman," Owen said.

"That's not the point. It's typical of Wyman to find contacts who are as extravagant as he is. Typical. Anyone else would have found a nice fat commissar who would settle for a couple of thousand and an easy defection. Not Wyman: he has to find some prima donna with gold fever."

Owen nodded sympathetically.

"It's unfortunate, I agree."

"Unfortunate? It's bloody outrageous. All I can say is, I'm damned glad we're not giving Wyman a pension. Who does he think he is, the last of the big-time spenders?"

"I'm sure the results will justify the cost."

"Nothing will justify the cost. Nothing. I keep saying it, but nobody will listen: there's an economic recession on."

CHAPTER FORTY-TWO

MARGARET RAMSEY WOKE UP AND got out of bed. She gazed sleepily out of the window at a pleasant spring morning. She put on her dressing gown, went into the kitchen and switched on the kettle. While the water boiled, she examined the letter-box.

There were two letters and a post-card. The first letter turned out to be a final demand on her electricity bill. The other letter was a glossy communication which told her that she had been chosen from thousands as the lucky person who could win a fortune in "Hegel's Lucky Draw Competition".

The electricity bill went into a drawer, and "Hegel's Lucky Draw Competition" was consigned to the dust-bin. She then read the postcard. On the front was a picturesque view of the Italian Alps. On the back was a small note printed in block capitals.

211

TURIN AIRPORT

JUNE 2 P.M.

DEAR MARGARET,

ALL'S WELL. THE WEATHER HERE IS LOVELY. I THINK YOU'D
REALLY ENJOY THE SCENERY. SEE YOU SOON.

LOVE,
BETTY.

She smiled and looked at the postmark. The card
had been sent on May 30. In that case, she wondered,
why had it been dated June 2? It then occurred to her
that June 2 was today's date.

"Of course!" she exclaimed.

Wyman meant her to fly out that day to Turin.

She telephoned British Airways and booked a seat
on the 2.30 flight to Turin. The "P.M." on the postcard
indicated that Wyman would be waiting for her that
afternoon.

She looked at her watch and estimated that she had
four hours to pack her things.

"Four hours!" she groaned. "Oh Michael, you are
impossible sometimes."

She lit a cigarette and made herself a coffee.

CHAPTER FORTY-THREE

RAWLS ARRIVED IN GENEVA on the morning of June 3. Like Wyman, he had little interest in the Swiss or their cities, so he went directly to his destination, the Banque Internationale Descartes.

He introduced himself to M. Piaget as Thompson Clarke of the US Internal Revenue Service, and he showed him the false identity papers that the Company had provided. Piaget studied them with suspicion.

"What can I do for you, Mr Clarke?"

"I am investigating the case of an American citizen who is clearly guilty of tax evasion. He is also known to be involved in other forms of organized crime in the United States, but for various reasons the authorities are concentrating on his tax evasion."

"I understand," Piaget said. "Is this person a client of our bank?"

"No," Rawls said. "However, a substantial sum of money illegally held by this man is being kept by one of your account holders. The person concerned isn't a US national, and our man thinks that by using his account the money will be safe. Nevertheless, your client is in illegal possession of the money."

"I see," Piaget said. "How do you know the money is being held here?"

"We don't know who the account holder is, but we do know the number of the account. G2H-17-493: I believe that is one of yours?"

"Yes. What would you like us to do?"

"The sum held here isn't of much interest to us," Rawls said. "The man we want has a number of such arrangements in other banks here, and some of the accounts are much larger. All we want is the name of the account holder and the address you send correspondence to. We understand this account was opened by an agent of your client, and we'd like that agent's particulars as well."

"In other words," Piaget said, "you are asking us to lift banking secrecy with regard to this account. That is a very serious request."

"I know," Rawls said.

"I do not think we can grant your request. You have said yourself that the account holder is not an American citizen. He therefore does not fall under your jurisdiction."

"No, but the money does if it was illegally obtained."

Piaget looked at Rawls coldly.

"I happen to know that this account contains no US dollars."

"The money was laundered," Rawls said. "It was converted into another currency in France before being deposited here."

"Indeed. That makes your case a little difficult, doesn't it, Mr Clarke? Let me see…the only right that your organization has to examine this account would be under the 1973 Swiss-American Treaty. I presume you know all about that?"

Rawls nodded.

"Now as I recall," Piaget said, "the treaty stipulates that the account holder must be proven to be involved in organized crime. It must also be shown that the investigators' evidence is not sufficient to allow prosecution for anything except tax evasion. I believe this is known as the 'Al Capone Syndrome'."

"Right," said Rawls.

"I am sure that you can establish all these things," Piaget said. "I don't doubt it for one moment. But you must first satisfy the officers of the Swiss National Bank and the Swiss police. Until you do that, I cannot lift the secrecy on this account."

"I know that," Rawls said, "and technically you're right. But for various reasons we want to avoid all that rigmarole. The person we're after is very highly placed, and if we began formal proceedings he'd probably hear about it. At the moment, he doesn't know we're onto him, and I'd like to keep it that way."

"I'm sure you would," Piaget smiled. "But I cannot afford to destroy the reputation of this bank merely to help the IRS with their investigations."

Rawls breathed out deeply and nodded.

"Okay, Mr Piaget. It looks like I'm going to have to

spell it out. In July '82, you and most other Swiss banks signed a document called—" he referred to some notes— "'The Convention on the Need for Caution when Accepting Deposits and on the Use of Banking Secrecy'. Some title, isn't it? As I say, you're a signatory to this, aren't you?"

"That is so," Piaget agreed. "What of it?"

"Article 9 of the Convention stipulates that you, the banks, must not assist with tax evasion, and Article 3 says that, quote, 'the identity of the beneficial owner should be checked with a care appropriate to the circumstances', unquote."

"I am aware of all this," Piaget said.

"Good," Rawls said. "Then you also know what the penalties are for infringing these articles. If an account beneficiary turned out to be a good old-fashioned crook with a hand in most forms of organized crime, it would probably be claimed that you didn't check up on him carefully enough. You'd be, quote, 'guilty of negligence leading to the appropriation of illegal funds', unquote. You could be up for a fine of ten million francs—that's what the Convention says, isn't it?"

"You have studied the Convention very carefully, Mr Clarke."

"It's my business to," Rawls lied. "And that isn't the end of it. If my Government decides that your bank was unwilling to co-operate with the US in stopping tax evasion, your assets in the US might be frozen. You do have assets in the US, don't you, Mr Piaget?"

"You know perfectly well we do," Piaget said frostily.

"Right," Rawls said. "So it's in everybody's interest for you to give me the information I want. Your bank's name won't be mentioned in any criminal proceedings, and no one will ever know about it except us. Your reputation will remain unblemished. How does that sound?"

"Very neat," Piaget said. "I will need a few moments to think about this."

"Sure."

Piaget leaned back in his leather-bound swivel chair and gazed at the ceiling in deep thought. After a few moments he said:

"Mr Clarke, we might be able to reach a satisfactory agreement without having to compromise the bank in any way."

"Yeah? How would we do that?"

"You work for the Internal Revenue Service. My client's agent suspected that this account might be the subject of inquiries by an American government organization, but not yours."

Rawls' eyes widened in surprise.

"Did he? And which organization did he have in mind?"

"I am not at liberty to say. But the agent was quite specific. He seemed to think that someone called Rawls might come here. Apparently Mr Rawls works for this organization."

"So?"

"We were instructed to keep a certain sealed document, which we were to give Mr Rawls if he appeared."

"Your client expected Rawls to trace his account?"

"Quite so," Piaget said. "It really is most extraordinary. However, we are accustomed to receiving extraordinary requests."

"I bet you are," Rawls said.

"The point is that our client seemed to think that Mr Rawls would be quite satisfied with the document, and that once he had read it, he would cease to investigate the account. Unfortunately, you are not Mr Rawls. You have identified yourself as Mr Clarke. However, if you were prepared to abandon all inquiries into this bank, and the account in question, I might be prepared to let you have the document."

"Got it," Rawls said.

"I would need your assurances that the matter would be regarded as closed, both by your organization and the other one. Are you in a position to make such an assurance on behalf of the other organization?"

"I am. They're also involved in this investigation."

"I thought so," Piaget said. "And what is your decision?"

"All right," Rawls said. "I'll take the document, and the bank won't be troubled by us again."

"Excellent," Piaget smiled. "If you will excuse me for one moment, I will fetch the document."

He left the room. Rawls' mind whirled with shock. How could anyone have expected him to arrive in Geneva? What the hell was going on?

Piaget returned, holding a long buff envelope in his bony hand. He gave it to Rawls, who opened it and drew out a typewritten letter. As he read the letter, Rawls went numb with surprise and confusion. Piaget watched him with detached interest.

"Is the document to your satisfaction?" he asked.

Rawls shook himself out of his trance, and forced himself to regain his composure.

"Yes," he stammered. "It's—it's most satisfactory. Thank you. I don't think there'll be anything else."

"Good," Piaget said. "I'm so glad. There is one more thing, Mr Clarke. Since the document was destined for a Mr Rawls, perhaps you could see to it that he receives it."

"Yes," Rawls said. "I'll—make sure he gets it. Thanks."

He pocketed the envelope and left M. Piaget's office, still numb with incredulity.

CHAPTER FORTY-FOUR

THE NORTH ITALIAN VILLAGE of Nirasca sits several thousand feet up in the Maritime Alps. Its bleached ochre streets and buildings have changed little in the last five hundred years. Hundreds of such villages are sprinkled across the region's grey-blue mountains, and Nirasca typifies their simple beauty and resistance to time. Tourists seldom visit the village, preferring to throng the crowded beaches of the Riviera some twenty miles to the south.

Wyman, however, had no desire to wallow in sweat and sun-tan lotion. He disliked tourists, and enjoyed the spacious serenity of the mountains.

He had first become acquainted with Nirasca some twenty-five years ago, when looking into the background of a suspected KGB plant in the Italian senate. The man had been a partisan in these mountains during the Second World War, and it was suspected that his contact with Communist resistance movements had led to his subornment by the Soviets.

Had the Senator stood as a Communist, or even a Socialist, there would have been little that anyone could do. But the man had been a Christian Democrat, and was tipped to be included in the next Government. Wyman had interviewed his friends and relatives in the village, and he established conclusively that the Senator was, in fact, a Communist. The information had been passed on to the Italian authorities, and the Senator was quietly expelled from the Christian Democrat party.

Since then, Wyman had visited the village a number of times, and had come to feel at home there.

On June 2 Margaret had arrived at Turin airport. They had driven down to Nirasca, and stayed at the village's tiny hotel, the *Albergo dei Santi*. Wyman no longer used the Ryle passport, and instead travelled under his own name.

"I suppose it's all over now," Margaret said.

"What is?" Wyman asked.

"You know, all that business with the Firm. They will leave us alone, won't they?"

"I think so. But there's one more matter to be resolved. Shall I get the coffee?"

They were sitting at a table outside a café in the village square. Wyman went inside to order two coffees while Margaret watched the villagers begin the day's business. It was a cool morning, but the cloudless sky presaged a hot afternoon. Wyman returned with coffee.

"What's this unfinished business?" Margaret asked.

"Yesterday I received a telegram from Geneva.

Apparently Rawls turned up at the Banque Descartes, as I suspected he would. I think we can expect him to arrive here any time."

"What does he want?"

"My head on a plate, I should think. I've put him to an awful lot of trouble, you know."

"Will he...will there be trouble?" Wyman smiled.

"I don't see why," he said. "I intend to be most hospitable."

Margaret stirred some sugar into her coffee.

"I hope you're right," she said doubtfully.

"Of course I'm right," Wyman grinned. He lit a cigarette and took a sip of coffee. "Up until very recently, Mr Rawls thought I was a harmless idiot. I suspect he has now revised his opinion of me."

"And if he hasn't?"

"Then it is Mr Rawls who is the idiot."

Margaret laughed and drank her coffee.

Five minutes later, a yellow Triumph Spitfire rolled into the square and parked by the café. A soberly dressed man with tinted spectacles got out of the car and walked to Wyman and Margaret.

"Good morning," Wyman said.

"Maybe," Rawls said. He was not smiling.

Wyman stood up politely and beamed affably at the American.

"May I introduce my fiancée? Mr Rawls—Margaret Ramsey."

"How do you do?" Margaret said.

"I don't do very well," Rawls snapped. "At least, not as well as your fiancé."

Margaret stiffened in embarrassment.

"I think I'll go for a walk," she said. "I'm sure you'd prefer to talk in private."

"Yes," Wyman said. "I'll be over for lunch at the hotel."

"Cheerio, then. Goodbye, Mr Rawls."

"Pleasure meeting you," Rawls said, not making it sound very pleasurable.

Margaret walked away.

"Can I get you a coffee?" Wyman said. "Or perhaps something stronger?"

"Just coffee," Rawls grunted.

He sat down and waited for Wyman to get the coffee.

"I must say," Wyman remarked as he returned, "you don't exactly look full of the joys of spring."

"That's because I'm not. In the last few weeks I've been thrown around the world, beaten up, and nearly had my ass shot off in Germany, just so you could sting the Firm for two million sterling. How would you feel?"

"You have my sympathy," Wyman said.

"Sure. I bet you cried all the way to the Banque Internationale Descartes."

"Did you visit Erfurt, then?"

"Yeah. Nearly got killed for my pains."

"You should have taken Major Bulgakov's advice."

Rawls' face lit up in surprise.

"You know Bulgakov?"

"Not intimately. He came round to my flat one evening and said that the search for a ferret in the Firm was a waste of time. Of course, I knew that better than anyone else, but I had to lead him along. He told me that he'd paid you a similar visit."

Rawls nodded and looked grimly at the nonchalant Wyman.

"I suppose you'd better tell me the whole story," he said. "I want to know how you set the whole thing up. And I want to know why your friends in Geneva were waiting for me to show up."

Wyman smiled and leaned back in his seat.

"I'm surprised that you haven't worked out most of it already. Perhaps you have, and you just want it confirmed. Anyway, the story runs as follows.

"I was responsible for the Grünbaum file, and I was therefore in a position to alter it. When Grünbaum was killed in a genuine accident, I obtained the names of various other people who'd been arrested in previous, wholly unrelated incidents. By adding their names to the file, I made it appear that members of Grünbaum's network had been blown before Grünbaum himself. Since this cannot happen with an F-network, it gave the impression that there was a Soviet infiltrator in London who was feeding network details back to Moscow Centre. I wanted the Firm to believe this, as I knew that I would be put in charge of the investigation.

"Of course, all those other arrests had nothing to do with Grünbaum, and those people had never even heard of him, but how was the Firm to know that? Their names were on the file, and that was all that was needed.

"As soon as Owen gave me the task of finding this mythical Soviet plant, I invented a new DDR contact, whom we code-named Plato. I explained to Owen that Plato was a well-placed informer who could discover the full circumstances of Grünbaum's arrest. However, Plato had not been suborned. He was a mercenary, and he would only supply the information we needed for an exorbitant fee: two million pounds. I was eventually entrusted with the money (since Plato would only deal with me) and having put the money in Geneva, here I am."

"Very cute," Rawls observed drily. "So why involve the Company in all this?"

"Thanks to the Government, the Firm has been forced to economize severely. Stations have been closed down or put on ice all over the world. People are being made redundant, and there's very little spare cash around. Even after I had tampered with the Grünbaum file, I knew it would be difficult to persuade my superiors to part with all that money."

"You mean they didn't believe you had a Moscow ferret?"

"They weren't sure and, under the circumstances, they preferred not to believe it. I needed something else to tip the scales, something that would convince them of the gravity of the situation.

"So I decided to bring you into it. I knew that if I got Frank Schofield to make inquiries in Rome, it would eventually get back to Langley. Given the Company's traditional doubts about security at the Firm, I knew you would want to find out what was going on. And I was right. When you arrived at Percy Street on the 21st, I was fully aware of what you were after. I couldn't believe my good fortune when you left your fingerprints all over the filing cabinet, and switched the typewriter ribbon."

"You checked all that out?" Rawls said incredulously.

"Oh yes. You see, I needed to prove that the Company was involved in the affair. Of course, I knew perfectly well that you were only snooping, but that wasn't the way I presented it to Owen.

"As far as my superiors were concerned, it was proof positive that you also knew we had a ferret in London, and that you were trying to track him down. Up until then, nobody wanted to believe that we had a Moscow plant, and nobody wanted to spend two million on Plato. Your arrival changed all that."

"I bet," Rawls said. "And Bulgakov's involvement made up their minds, I guess."

"Bulgakov was a positive godsend. He knew about my first trip to Europe, and he knew about your arrival. I suppose he couldn't keep his nose out of it, but when he became involved it set everybody's mind racing."

Wyman lit a cigarette and blew out a long trail of smoke.

"What happened in Germany?" he asked.

"I nearly got killed, that's what happened. Bulgakov warned me away, so I figured he had something to hide. I snooped around in Erfurt, and found out that Neumann was a real nut after all. That was your best move, Wyman. Everybody thinks that Communist mental hospitals are full of sane dissidents. Nobody ever stops to think that they've got real screwballs too. When I found out the truth about Neumann, things started to click. Then I was taken by some of Bulgakov's friends, and they threw me out of the country. Bulgakov thinks the whole thing's a real scream."

"I'm sure he does," Wyman grinned.

Rawls shook his head.

"I still don't get it," he said. "How did you know I'd get to Geneva?"

"The typewriter ribbon," Wyman said. "I'd typed all my memos to Owen on it. I also wrote a few notes of my own on it, and when I realized you'd exchanged the ribbon, I guessed that you would find out about the bank account. That didn't bother me too much, since I'd already laid my plans. It was known that I was the agent for the account, and therefore it would be presumed that the beneficial owner was somebody else: the elusive Plato. But nobody knew that I had opened the account with a false passport, and that the beneficial owner was Michael Wyman.

"Hence, it would only be a question of time before you appeared in Geneva to force the bank into giving you Plato's identity. I wanted you to try it, so that you would get my letter and come here."

"Why?"

"I want you to tell my former masters what has happened. You must explain to them that there is no infiltrator in the Firm, as far as I know, and that Plato does not exist. My dealings with the Firm are finished—you must make that quite clear."

"Why me? Why not tell them yourself?"

"They probably wouldn't believe me. They were seldom inclined to believe me when I was employed by them, so I doubt if they would believe me now. Besides, it will sound better coming from a disinterested party like yourself."

"They'll want their money back."

"They can't have it."

"They'll kill you for it."

"No." Wyman shook his head emphatically.

"What makes you think you're safe? They can send out a hitman any time they like. And there's your fiancée…"

"No," Wyman repeated. "There's an added twist. You see, I'm not quite the happy imbecile I've been taken for. I have placed signed documents in the hands of various European lawyers. These documents explain all that has happened, in minute detail. Should anything happen to me, or my fiancée, these documents will be given to the editors of certain left-wing European publications that have little sympathy for Britain.

"I'm sure you can imagine what would happen if this story were published. The Firm would be internationally disgraced, and the Government would have a lot of talking to do. I'd be obliged if you explained all this to the Firm when you see them. Owen will be delighted."

Rawls gazed at Wyman in silence for a few moments. He found it hard to credit the Englishman with the sort of ingenuity he clearly possessed. Wyman looked and sounded like a plump, overgrown schoolboy. It occurred to Rawls that Wyman's success lay entirely in his ability to convince others of his own ineptitude and harmlessness. Rawls' face creased into a broad grin.

"Shit!" he exclaimed. "You've really screwed them, haven't you?"

Wyman nodded solemnly.

"One more thing," Rawls said. "Why did you do it? Maybe that's a stupid question, but I don't understand."

"You wouldn't. And I'm not sure if I can explain it to you properly."

"Try me. You owe me that much."

"Very well. I've no doubt that you've read the file on me quite carefully. You know that I'm an academic, and that I've served the Firm faithfully for about thirty years.

"To spend a lifetime in both these fields, one must have a belief—no, 'belief' isn't a good word for it, that implies something conscious. Let's call it a deeply imbedded assumption about what one is doing, and why one does it. You might call it patriotism, but it's nothing so crude."

"I think I know what you mean."

"I hope so, because it isn't easy to describe one's most fundamental convictions. Individual opinions about single issues: those are easy to explain. But the fundamental source of all those opinions—the wellspring of one's ideas and beliefs—how do you explain that? It's an interesting epistemological dilemma."

Rawls coughed uncomfortably.

"I'm sorry," Wyman smiled. "I'll put it this way: I believed in a particular scheme of things, a system, if you like. I believed that this system went beyond trifling questions of money and power. What mattered most, as far as I was concerned, was that the system took care of its own, and loyalty was repaid with loyalty. And above all, Mr Rawls, the system *worked*. We governed nations with it, we won wars with it, and we knew it was the envy of the world. It was just and reasonable, and it spawned some of the finest minds on this planet."

"Yeah," Rawls said. "I've heard all that before somewhere."

Wyman laughed.

"I know. But unlike the politicians who put such

phrases in their speeches, I genuinely believed it all. I never actually *stated* these opinions, because I regarded them as self-evident truths. And then, just a few weeks ago, reality caught up with me."

"You mean you got fired. So what?"

"That's right, but it wasn't simply a question of 'getting fired'. It was made clear to me that I was no longer of any use to anyone. I was treated with all the sympathy and consideration that one affords a used contraceptive. There was no recognition of my work or loyalty, merely a desire to be rid of a spent component. I was hurt and insulted."

"So you got your revenge by creaming your people for two million. That's what I call an eye for an eye."

"I can't defend my actions on moral grounds, and I admit that I wanted to exact some form of vengeance. That may be puerile, but if you rob someone of the moral framework they've lived by for nearly sixty years, you must expect them to behave amorally, I think.

"Besides, there were other considerations. My fiancée is expecting a child, and I still have alimony to pay on my last marriage. Since I'm not receiving a pension from either the Firm or my College, my conscience won't be too troubled by what I've done. Does that explain my motives, Mr Rawls?"

"I guess so. I've got a feeling one or two other people are going to be fired over this."

"Perhaps," Wyman said.

"That doesn't bother you?"

"It bothers me slightly less than my predicament bothered them. The only person I owe an apology to is yourself. I've put you to a lot of trouble and expense, and there isn't much I can do except offer you my heartfelt apologies. And a drink."

Rawls leaned back and grinned sheepishly.

"Okay," he said. "Whisky and soda, and we'll call it quits."

"Splendid," Wyman said, and they both laughed.

EPILOGUE

OWEN PUT DOWN the telephone receiver and stared blankly at the opposite wall. He took a couple of paracetamol and suppressed an urge to vomit all over his desk.

"The bastard," he croaked. "The utter bastard."

He tried to collect his thoughts, but nothing fully registered. Wyman had invented the whole story—it was a total fiction. He had stolen the two million pounds and was now completely untouchable. He had deceived everybody and walked off scot-free. He had humiliated Owen and the Minister in the eyes of the Prime Minister and the Americans. And the worst of it was, he probably couldn't care less.

"The bastard," Owen repeated. "How could he?"

It occurred to Owen that Wyman had not just done this for the money. He had wanted to disgrace the Firm;

he had taken revenge in the form of an elaborate, and expensive, practical joke.

"The utter bastard," Owen said. Shock seemed to limit his vocabulary.

He pressed a button on his intercom and asked for a cup of tea.

He looked out of the window and shook his head. Where had they gone wrong?

There was, he reflected, one small crumb of consolation in all this. The original panic could now be forgotten: there really was no infiltrator in MI6. He sighed in relief as Mrs Hobbes walked in.

"Here's your tea, Mr Owen," she said. "White, no sugar."